#minithology

MOONLIT WINGS

EDITED BY   N.D. GRAY

featuring

TRACY EIRE   ELIZABETH KNOLLSTON   EMBER FANE

KARLI STITES   HEIDI MOONE

CONTENTS

INTRODUCTION

NIGHT. THE MOON RISING WHILE the world holds its breath. In the stillness, the sound of wings.

We lift our face, eyes wide. Search the sky. Listen with our entire being.

What is out there?

Whether it is an owl swooping low, or a crane high above, or a bat looping-a-loop to catch insects, the sound of moonlit wings is magical. Encounters of wonder. Invoking a sense of other.

If we are lucky enough to have such an experience, it is a moment of poetry, of enchantment. Of peace and power. A chance meeting we press in the memory book of our hearts. Encounters we sketch with pen and ink and words into our journals or memoirs.

The stories in this #minithology are spun out from such powerful moments. Set in places as diverse as a city theater, the sky above a Civil War battle, or deep in a magical forest, our stories, quite unplanned, share the theme of becoming.

Our main characters are required to risk, to stretch, to break open and *become*. To soar to heights they had not hitherto known.

Embrace the night.

Embrace the magic.

Fly with us on moonlit wings.

ND Gray

September 2021

Camp Verde, AZ

Ember Fane would choose elemental wings if she could have a functional set of her own. While wings shaped from fire and ice and stardust seem farfetched, they are no less than wings of feathers for a human.

She combines both feathers and magic to give us a story of transformation beneath the moonlight. A story of loyalty and sacrifice. A tale of Bone Crows and the things we are willing to become so others need never face such a choice

LITTLE CROW

EMBER FANE

In the dark, should they meet you,

The Bone Crows will surely eat you.

THESE WERE THE WORDS THE children chanted on the day Cora began her transformation.

Carry lamp and carry candle,

Carry basket without handle.

She was one of the chanting children, just on the edge of too old for skipping games.

Tip it o'er their bony head,

Tip it fast or you'll be dead.

Brown skirts swishing around her knees and loose hair tangled about her shoulders, Cora skipped–

Right foot.

Right foot.

Left foot.

Both.

Hopping away from the front of the line, she made room for her younger cousin who followed behind.

Elsie had a streak of dirt on her forehead and a pert, freckle-dusted nose. The sunlight played over her spun-blond curls. Liquid blue eyes shining, she hopped with both feet together to counteract her twisted right foot. Panting with the effort, she made the last jump. Hobbling only slightly, she went to stand at Cora's side, as Riya, Tami, and Del finished the skipping rhyme.

While the children chanted, the wind rippled the stalks of wheat just beyond the pasture behind the thatched-roof log barn. Though they were used to playing farther afield, the last few weeks the grown-ups had required they remain close to home. They could go no farther than the end of the oblong swath of green grasses running between the barn and the cluster of houses in the farming hamlet.

The children didn't know why, only that their parents whispered anxiously each evening. Quietly speaking of things that should not be named. In the bright afternoon, such foreboding whispers seemed far away. White and yellow and greenish-blue butterflies fluttered here and there. Above, a flock of sparrows wheeled through the blue sky. The aroma of spices in the evening stew—now beginning to warm on the hearths—drifted across the green grass, mingling with the scent of sun-warmed hay.

Like the barn, the low, wide dwellings of the hamlet were log and thatch. Built long, they accommodated three or more families. One home had a door the color of a summer sun. Another, a deep, spring green. Other doors were marigold, or rose, or snow. Bright spots in the work-a-day life of the field hands and housewives. Flowers grew in boxes before the low windows, and Ole Nan, the milk goat, stood on top of one of the houses, queen of all she surveyed.

It was an afternoon of exquisite peace, the kind children do not notice, because to them, all is as it should be. They were two dozen strong as they lined up and skipped again, this time to Joni Go Home. Then, Star-man Riding and Stoke the Fire. They had a stone throwing competition and made whistles from blades of grass. After an avid discussion about when the traveling tinker was due—a tinker known to bring peppermint sweets—they began another skipping game.

As she recited the rhyme and skipped the familiar steps, Cora felt unease steal over her. She could not say where the ill feeling came from, just that a dark cloud dimmed the sun. Something heavy crawled into her bones and made her more aware of the world than she had ever been. More aware of the summer heat. The flecks of hay dancing in the sunbeams. The feeling of the world—as if it were a ripe melon set to burst. Or to sour in on itself.

Little crow, little crow,

Heed the path where you go.

Spread your wings, learn to fly,

Become you, or you'll die.

Feather's black, eyes that shine,

Who are you? Is this your time?

Little crow, little crow

Who you are—the bones know.

She hesitated at the end of the complex sequence of skips, watching Elsie out of the side of her eye. The younger girl made the last jump with both feet and smiled at Cora.

In the cluster of children who had already finished, someone whispered, "Doesn't count."

Elsie looked down at her feet, shoving the right one deeper into the grass so as to hide the two missing toes and the odd twist where the arch of the foot went inward.

While Elsie looked down, Cora looked up, eyes narrowing as she attempted to ferret out who had made the comment. Pugle's jaw was set and he was the only one who met Cora's eye. "Why's that, Pugsie?" she asked, voice sharp as talons.

Though younger than both girls, the boy didn't back down. He stabbed a finger at Elsie in a gesture that mirrored ones his father made. "She used both feet. Doesn't count."

"Say that again and I'll bloody your nose." Cora's hands balled into fists and she stepped away from the others, ready to mind Pugle some manners. For his part, the boy's jaw thrust out farther and he set his feet to charge.

But at that moment, Del finished the game, hopping off to the side of the grass patch, his bare feet slapping the ground. His hop was immediately followed by a sound like thunder rolling over the fields. The air tingled, tasting strange when Cora licked her lips.

"Bone Crows are coming," whispered Riya.

Elsie's older sister, Viyat, nodded agreement. "Maman says the thunder rolls too much without rain, these days."

Rainless thunder *had* rolled often in recent weeks, but Cora's papa had quieted his family's concerns by explaining it was just the far away clouds shifting in the sky. That they pushed the thunder before them and so, soon, the summer showers would come. They would sweep over the forest and woods, then out onto the fields. The raindrops would patter down onto the thatch and Ole Nan would run under the eaves to save herself a drenching.

"It might be *bolgken neevies*," Del said. "Trampling through the woods and belching."

"Hush, Del," his twin, Tami, punched him on the arm. "You know maman said papa was only trying to frighten us with that story and that he shouldn't have named them at all."

"Nah." Her brother shook his head, a thick lock of dark hair falling over his eyes. "I heard Daril talkin' to Koon about the tracks they found in the western pastures. He said nothing natural made 'em."

Riya snorted her derision. "*Neevies* will only kill us dead. But, the Bone

Crows will eat us." She cocked her head and stared down at Elsie. "They like littles best."

"Stop," Cora commanded, reaching out to touch Elsie's shoulder. The younger girl's eyes were wide and round. Cora, too, felt the fingers of cold horror stroking the bumps along her spine, but she masked her fear with a burning glare.

"You know the stories," Riya retorted. "You heard the rainless thunder. That's the sound the world makes when one of them–" She cut off, her face registering surprise as she looked over Cora's shoulder. Then, the blood drained out of her sun-tanned cheeks.

Fear danced along Cora's arms as she turned slowly to look at what had frightened Riya so. Could it be a pod of *neevies* crawling toward them straight from a tinker's tale? She imagined their eyes glinting wickedly, pinchers snapping the air, saliva stringing between their razor-sharp teeth, their snake tails whipping violently.

It was not monsters crawling through the fields. Only a man in a black cloak. He led two horses—a large roan and a thorn gray. On his shoulder rode a bone white bird. The sun glinted off the magic, silver chain running from the cuff on the bird's leg and the silver armband around his upper arm. Half a field separated the pair from the group of the children and, already, Riya and Del were in flight. Running toward the houses. Elsie pulled away from Cora and joined them, Tami quick on her heels, and then, leaving her behind.

Cora lingered, though her feet edged of their own accord toward home. Despite his tall and muscular build, she barely spared a glance for the man.

It was the bird she watched. Sunlight seemed to make the bird's face burn with white heat bordered by dark fire. Through the heat, across the distance, the Bone Crow caught and held Cora's eyes for a long moment of time, which spun out in breathless, heart-beat-less silence.

Cora shuddered. The spell broke. She, too, ran.

CORA AND THE OTHERS DID not stop running until they had reached the far side of the long green where Viyat had already called her mother out of their house. Aunt Ingra held her youngest in her arms, a chubby, squirming babe. Ruffling her son's curls, she looked over the children's heads at the approaching man.

Arms dusted with flour and holding herb twine and the hamlet's only pair of shears, Pon appeared in the doorway of the house where the unmarried men lived. Pon was cook and caretaker and kept the men from turning the place into a sty. He also had an unerring nose for gossip.

For a moment, it appeared the man and horses would come directly to the houses, but from somewhere to the east an unearthly scream rent the afternoon's peace. The harsh sound lasted for ten heartbeats and lingered in the air.

Doors clattered against walls as mothers came running, the names of their children tumbling over one another. Without hesitation, the cloaked man sprang up onto the roan horse and rode toward the sound.

The crow on his shoulder fell off to the side. Her wings snapped open. Beat downward. Black, magic smoke swirled round and round. Trailed the crow as she rose high into the air. Soon, the Bone Crow was above and before the man. The thin, silver chain stretching out between them sparkled as it caught the sunlight.

The two disappeared on the far side of Pon's house and Cora, without thinking, gathered up her skirts and ran down the furrows of the vegetable garden laid out between the long houses.

She didn't hear her mother call her name. She didn't notice the ripening tomatoes or bright squash or the gourd cages. Her eyes were fixed on the tree line beyond the pasture. And the fields beyond them, where another unearthly cry screamed through the air sounding as if someone were trying to saw a bolt of lightning in half.

No animal, not even one in gravest pain, could sound like that. She had to know what it was.

Grasping the thin, wooden railings in each hand, she clambered up over the stile and raced across the rich green pasture. The six large oxen within the enclosure had clustered together at the far end and they watched her nervously.

The man on the horse had been forced around the pasture by the fence, so Cora beat him to the tree line. Sharp edges bit into the balls of her feet as she climbed up the fence.

Horse and rider went past with a jangle of harness and the smell of sweat and leather. Up close, there was no mistaking the silver crown insignia on the clasp of his cloak or on the pommel of his sword sheathed behind his saddle. He was, indeed, a Guardian of a Bone Crow. Protector of one of the King's Witches.

He spared Cora not a glance as he spurred the roan forward, the thorn gray loping behind.

She waited for the second horse to pass, then dropped to the ground and ran through a copse of close-growing birches.

Above them, the Bone Crow circled the field where Cora's father and the other farmers were trampling the early wheat around a large hole in the ground. Half in and half out of the hole, an enormous creature writhed and thrashed.

It was as if tree roots had heard of squash slugs and decided to create one. The bulbous creature opened its mouth and a fleshy tree-root tongue peeked out.

The sight brought Cora up short. She bent, panting, hands braced on knees but unable to look away.

There was no *bolgken* like this in any of the stories she had ever heard.

Another grating scream filled the air.

The field hands slashed at the root-slug with their scythes and stabbed with their pitchforks. Her papa, Melor, was among the workers, shouting encouragement to his friend and curses at the creature as they faced it down.

Without slowing, the Guardian shouted instructions at the workers while leaping from his horse, which ran on, only to circle around before the farthest side of the field. It did not return, but pranced back and forth, blowing great breaths through its nose and tossing its head at the thorn gray trotting through the wheat well away from the chaos.

Sword held in both hands, the Guardian inserted himself between the root-slug and the workers. They backed away but did not abandon the lone figure balancing on the balls of his feet.

Above the tableau, the Crow cawed a challenge.

Cora felt the Crow's cry from deep inside her own self. It made her toes curl and her fingertips itch. It made her lips draw back from her teeth. It gave her nightmares of flying.

The Crow dove. Beak open. Talons stretching for a strike. Wings spread. And spreading. And…

Spreading.

The smoky magic filled the spaces between her white feathers, becoming black feathers. And gray and blue and bone. Until the crow was as large as a horse and thrice as dangerous.

Beak, and talons, and bone blades along her wings' leading edge—all found their targets as the Bone Crow whirled and spun, lifted into the air on wings of magic, only to drop again and again on the root slug. Twisted root appendages thrust out, attempting to spear the crow, but she altered her size and danced among them, leaving severed roots behind.

A soft gasp caught Cora's attention and she looked over to see Elsie standing nearby, eyes wide and shining as she watched the Guardian inflict his own portion of damage, great sword flashing in the afternoon light.

Together, the cousins watched the King's Witch and her Guardian strike at the unknown *bolgken* until it lay unmoving, its body heaped out of its hole.

"What is it?" Elsie asked, only now moving to stand immediately beside Cora who shook her head in admission of ignorance.

"Where are the others?" Cora asked as they watched the Guardian embed his sword deep inside the front part of the root-slug. Green tar oozed out.

"Sent inside," Elsie replied, her nose wrinkling at the stench that carried across the field from the oozing tar. "I went in while they were shouting for you and I came out the back door before they knew it." She flashed a grin at her own cleverness, but sobered as the Bone Crow, still as large as a horse, landed on top of the root-slug's carcass.

The Bone Crow hissed, twisting her head from side to side, eyeballing each of workers.

"Control your Witch," the girls heard Pugly's father say.

"She is caught up in the Frenzy and your scythes make her nervous. Back away slowly."

The Guardian had not turned his head to reply, but fixed his gaze on the Witch. Now he transferred his sword to his left hand and wrapped his right around the chain. He began to speak in a language Cora had only heard mentioned in tales. The language of the Guardians.

He spoke firmly, but gently, and Cora imagined he was telling the Witch how good she was. See? They had defeated the root-slug. But the people were not to be harmed.

"He's telling her not to allow the magic to win," Elsie whispered. "Like in the story of Ishyla. He's asking her to remember herself."

One large talon pierced the root-slug carcass and ripped up a pumpkin-sized piece. Holding it in the air, the Bone Crow twisted her neck to the side and slowly lowered her head.

The Guardian nodded and spoke so they could all hear. "Yes. Eat."

Catching the flesh in her beak, she tilted her head back and swallowed, before stabbing into the carcass again. This time, more of the green tar oozed out, and with it, a black mist. The *satha* which had given the creature its life.

Cora wondered what it would be like to have such power—power to destroy a *bolgken* and eat the very magic which animated it. And yet, to be so helpless. To be dependent on someone else to remember who you were. To call you back to yourself when the magic threatened to tear you away. To prevent you from seeing your friends and family as enemies, the carcasses of which were ripe for eating.

Even if the Goddess asked in person, she could never chose to be a Bone Crow.

THEY PLACED BROAD PLANKS OF wood upon sawhorses in the center of the hamlet that had no name. The evening meals were brought out, arranged in no particular order, and it was a matter of luck from which pot the diners were served. With the last of the sun's rays slanting over them, the people from the farming hamlet clutched their carved spoons and the thick, fired-clay plates spun out on Marin's wheel down at Bridgeturn, the farthest away from home Cora had ever been.

Sweaty faces and dirty hands had been scrubbed raw. Hair and beards combed. Their best clothes donned, no matter that they were plainly cut, homespun, hand-sewn, and would be next year's workaday clothes.

They gathered like this in honor of the King's Witch and her Guardian. When all was ready, the bone white crow leapt from the man's shoulder to the ground. When she landed, a woman stood there. Calmly composed, looking the farthest thing from the half-*bolgken* monster that might have eaten them had her Guardian not been there to stop her.

The Witch wore a traveling uniform. Bone white boots mostly hidden under wide, white trousers. A matching coat—long in back, short in front—was worn over a blouse. A bone white mask covered the upper portion of her face. Black feathers spread out from the edges of the mask and lay along her auburn hair. Black tassels were tied around her upper arms, one of them draped over the silver circlet. It was a marvel the way the thin chain hanging from the circlet waxed and waned with her movements, so that it was always attached to her and her Guardian but it never became a hindrance in their activities.

It was the mask that held Cora's attention. There was a sheen to it, as if it were rubbed in oil. The part over the nose was made to look like the gracefully—though dangerous—curved beak of a bird. The entire thing seemed to move with her face. The Witch didn't smile. She didn't quite express any emotion, but the small movements of her face—the mask did not hide them. It accented.

The black feathers held Power. They smoked occasionally, a black smoke that coiled around the vanes and lazily lifted away, only to draw down into other feathers. Cora had seen that Power in action and she watched it now. Wondering. In awe... And yet with a sick twist in her guts. If the stories were true....

The duo sat at Yardley's table. On Yardley's best chairs. The man himself was perched on a stool. His beard twitching, he made a valiant effort at conversation with the Guardian, a man stern of face and economical of movement whose name was Sardos.

Sardos had tossed his black cloak behind his shoulders, but his uniform was no less imposing. The scarlet and purple medal over his heart bore the King's medal of Valor, adding weight to his presence, if the afternoon's battle had not carried enough of its own.

Everyone was silent as they ate, so they clearly heard Yardley stumble over his thanks for the battle well fought and his question on the nature of the *bolgken* which had erupted out of their field.

No one had been hurt, though Daril would be laid up for a time with a twisted ankle. That they had all survived was a praise that fell from everyone's lips. The small flower garden east of the hamlet would be tended well in the weeks to come, with many a little gift left to show appreciation to the goddess of the fields and forests for her protection.

It was the Witch who answered Yardley's question, her cool voice carrying over them like the breeze before a storm. "A young *bolgken mattentalg.*"

"It is rare," Guardian Sardos replied. "*Mattentalg* burrow to lay eggs. The young remain buried, soaking up *satha* until they have grown. Then they come forth."

"Was it something we did that awakened this one?" Yardley asked. "And are there more?"

"Nothing," the Witch answered, but her eyes scanned the gathered people and Cora thought it was as if the Witch sought something only she could see. Further evidence that the stories were true? "We will call for my Sisters to join us. We will seek beneath your fields and forests for more."

There were murmurs as everyone envisioned their harvest destroyed by a cadre of Bone Witches trampling over the fields, the Witches and their hungering Power leashed only by fine silver chains.

"We'll be happy to offer you a guide, Mistress," Yardley offered, sweat breaking out on his forehead. "To ease your search. Koon is a strong tracker. He knows the land and can guide you around the old quarries. Deep pools of dark water they are. No place for you, Mistress. Not that you would lose your way, of course. No offense meant."

Yardley was rambling, unable to stop his words under the cool gaze of the Witch which seemed to say he had no idea what sorts of places were for her.

The conversation faded for Cora. She hadn't touched her stew and fresh bread which were growing cold upon her plate. Instead of eating, she peered between the shoulders of the others to watch the King's Witch as she spoke with Yardley. The woman's movements were graceful and sure. She often reached for her glass of wine without looking—and without knocking it over, Cora noted.

She saw Elsie peeping between shoulders as well, her wide eyes captivated by the Guardian's great sword in its coal-black scabbard, which he had leaned against the table's end. Aunt Ingra tapped the girl on the shoulder and pointed at her plate. At the same time, Cora's mother hissed at her, "Coralae, cease your staring and eat."

Unable to force the food down her tight throat, Cora pushed a lump of potato from one side of her plate to another, maneuvering it among the other root vegetables and a couple of lumps of goat.

Riya was standing beside Cora and she leaned closer. "Fatten up. The Bone Crow needs to eat you." She giggled but it was a shaky giggle betraying her nervousness.

A dark look from her own maman silenced her, but Riya's words made Cora wonder—where had the rhyme come from? Did the King's Witches, the Bone Crows, *really* eat children as the tales told? Or were those stories meant to scare the littles and keep them from wandering too far from home?

During the clean up after the meal, when it was her turn to amuse Tam, Elsie's youngest brother, Cora made sure to hold him close and stay as far away from the Bone Crow as possible. Tam giggled in her arms, patting her chin with his fat little fingers.

They gave the King's Witch and her Guardian use of Talma and Hedley's rooms, and the newlyweds went across the green to stay with her parents. Sardos thanked them and, Crow on his shoulder, entered the dwelling and shut the door firmly behind them.

Cora lay in bed after everyone else was asleep and thought of root-slugs and darker *bolgken* that filled the stories, the ones spoken quietly, as if the naming of the creatures would call them forth.

She thought of Ishyla's Bargain with the Goddess. The only way to save the world from destruction. Of being doomed to the fate of the Bone Crow—nay, *choosing* that fate when the Goddess called—as Ishyla had done for herself. And Cora shuddered.

As she drifted off to sleep, her arms opened wide. Her fingers spread and she dreamed of black plumes of Power wafting around her. Of the joy of flight and the ability to fight the dark things that haunted the world.

In the night, the thunder rolled.

FOUR OTHER WITCHING PAIRS ARRIVED. One was a male, a rarity in the Sisterhood. They pitched tents on the green and watched over the harvest of the early wheat. The pairs even helped as they could.

When the fields were empty, the Witches transformed and burrowed into the ground where they found four more *mattentalg* and a dozen eggs. As their Guardians watched over them, the Bone Crows feasted on the *bolgken*, devouring the *satha*.

Cora had not seen this, nor had any other child. They had all been kept inside behind closed doors. But she listened to her parent's quiet conversations in the evenings. During the day, she and other children compared snatches of overheard conversations, piecing together a fairly accurate sequence of events.

After the Crows finished their feasting, the people of the nameless hamlet burned the dried *mattentalg* husks, forever rendering that particular field useless for planting.

Once they were certain the fields were empty of *mattentalgs*, the Witching pairs slipped away as quietly as they had come, Sardos and his Crow last of all. Then, the hamlet breathed a sigh of relief and life inched toward normal. The late crop was hurriedly planted. Even the children helped, their morning chores stretching into the afternoon, replacing skipping games for a time.

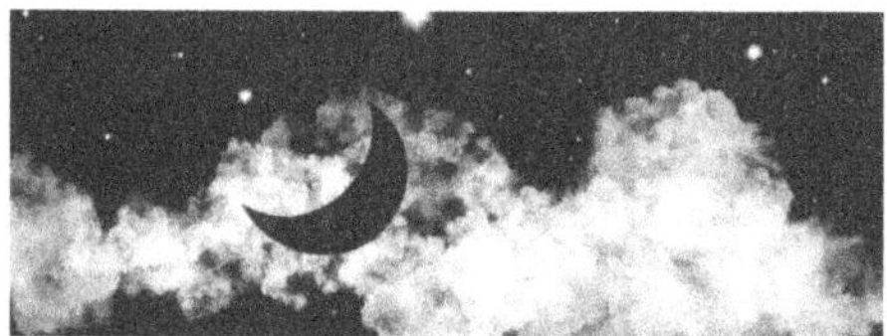

SLEEPING AT THE TABLE?" MAMAN'S gentle question brought her out of her reverie.

Cora was sitting at the heavy wooden table with her back to the wide kitchen hearth built from rocks brought up from the deep quarries to the south. Planks of wood fastened to the whitewashed log walls held the family's pottery. Beneath the shelves, a clay pitcher of water stood beside a ceramic basin where they washed their hands and dishes.

"Not feeling well?" Maman placed the back of her hand to Cora's forehead.

"My head hurts." Her voice sounded thick. "And my shoulders ache."

"Elsie is not well either. Crawl into the snug," Maman said and muttered curses over the Bone Crows under her breath.

Mouth feeling as if it were stuffed with cotton, Cora slowly climbed into the snug—a small platform and hay mattress covered in brightly colored summer quilts tucked between the stones of the large kitchen hearth and the smaller fireplace in Papa and Maman's bedroom.

It was warm in the little space. She pulled one of the thin quilts around her shoulders and lay her head on an arm. A moment later, Maman brought a spoonful of allsome tincture. The sweetly bitter medicine filled the snug with the scents of crushed herbs and old apples.

Soon, Cora drifted off into a heavy sleep.

Maman woke her several times. She clucked her tongue each time she touched the back of her hand to Cora's forehead. She spooned broth into Cora's mouth. The broth briefly washed away the cottony feeling that coated Cora's tongue and cheeks. Maman rubbed her back and, when she did, it felt like she was pushing little thorns into Cora's skin.

Once, after Maman gave Cora some broth, she changed out the summer quilts and one was stained with blood. Another time, a small, black feather fell out of the folds of the quilt with the blue and green clouds. Maman pressed a hand to her mouth, dropped the quilt, and picked up the feather in trembling fingers.

Some time later, Cora heard her parents whispering. Something had happened to Ole Nan. Some *thing* had gotten her. Cora tried to ask what it was. Had a *neevie* come from the deep woods? But her mouth was stuffed with feather dust and cold talons were piercing her skull.

Then, maman was crying—trying to do so quietly, but sobbing so hard she could barely catch her breath. "My baby. My baby. Not my only baby."

It was after this that Cora found herself floating through the air.

"Melor." Maman gasped the name, and it was Papa who replied. "It is a kindness. Do you want her to grow up *one of them*? We'll say she was delirious. She wandered out. Whatever took Ole Nan took her."

Maman had no other words, only sobs that cut off as something thudded dully in the dark.

As Cora floated through the air, she heard footsteps. Boots ground in the grass and dirt along the border of the fields where night peepers croaked their songs.

She floated downhill; the footsteps following her.

It came into her mind that she was being cradled, carried like a child swaddled in her blankets. The scent of soap and grass and dirt was around her, the smells associated with her Papa. Her head resting on his shoulder.

They entered the woods and twigs snapped beneath his boots.

She might have dozed off. Maybe not. It was a while before Papa put her down. He said nothing, but drew the quilts around her shoulders and her head. She felt him securing them around her shoulders, body, legs, and feet beneath which he knotted off the rope he'd wound around her.

Afterward, he touched her head. His palms resting like a blessing, a benediction, on her sweat-damp hair. A heartbeat the gentle touch remained.

"Damn the Goddess," he whispered. Then, his work-worn hands were placed against her side and Papa shoved her.

She was airborne once again. For a long moment she floated among the stars, the cool light of the moon giving her wings. Then she was falling.

Falling.

Falling into pure cold.

Freezing water opened up and swallowed her.

She sank.

Down.

Down.

The cold shocked her awake, but it was instinct that drove her. She twisted within the blanket. Writhed as the cold water filled her mouth and nose. Sought escape from the cocoon of quilt and water.

Suffocating, she heard the whispers but not the words. Understood a meaning but not the details. She had said "a never" but had she meant it? If she did, she need only wait a minute more. Wait until the breath in her body had been used up. Until the quarry had become her grave.

Or...

She could live.

Live her life in service to the Goddess, but live.

Faced with a watery death, her brave words washed away.

The light of the moon broke through the dark water. The whispers calling her.

She lifted her face toward the moonlight. Accepted the bargain.

The upper part of the blanket blossomed like a flower, floating around her like crinkled petals. Her hair lifted, fanning out into dandelion strands. She shrugged one arm free of the rope and quilts and reached upward. Something heavy at the end of the rope pulled her down.

She clawed the dark water. Clawed the quilts. Clawed them away from her.

Her burning lungs tried to breathe, and she inhaled water. In a frenzy, her legs sought freedom. Her arms swam. She tried to gain the surface but only sank deeper.

Then something inside of her felt like it was tearing open. She screamed out the last of the oxygen.

Her body went rigid.

The world paused.

Terrible flashes of light pierced the water, blinding through the eyelids she had squeezed shut. Then, her feet were free and she was rising.

Rising.

Rising.

The moment she broke the surface, the air hit her face. The oxygen poured into her in dizzying waves. Her stomach clenched as her body simultaneously tried to breathe and cough.

And still she rose.

But.... That wasn't right. That couldn't be. She threw herself at the nearest tree to prevent a second fall. She landed on a branch. Her entire body shook as she tried to look at her own feet.

Her eyes didn't work the way they should. She blinked. Squinted. Tried to bring things into focus. Not until she turned her head and used one eye did she see the bird feet beneath her body.

Bone white claws clutched the night dark bark.

A cool breeze blew over her ruffling feathers.

She shivered. Her entire body trembled, and she realized just how tiny she was. Unsure of anything, feeling as if she were dreaming, and still trying to catch her breath, she inched down the branch to huddle against the trunk of the tree.

The world turned, and the moon traced its arch across the sky, shining down onto the old quarry that had filled with water over the years.

It shone on the branch where Cora huddled. It shone on the bone white feathers and the black smoke which covered her head. The black smoke which drifted down and wrapped around her, warming her.

It shown on the dark forest and the *bolgken* moving through the trees on the far side of the quarry. Shadows great and small, made of twisted things, of smoke and roots and the leftover broken pieces of sky from the world that was here before the Goddess wove this one into existence. Cora shivered, as much at the sight of *bolgken* she'd never known existed before as she did at her own plight.

A couple of hours later, the moon was still in the sky, and she had stopped shivering. The newness and the fear easing enough she could notice the strange pulling inside of her. The sense that something was wrong. The whispers urging her onward....

Launching herself off the branch, she opened her wings and glided away from the tree and over the grassy spot where her father had tried to drown her. The memory of his hands pushing her flashed through her mind, along with the knowledge that she was now a bird in the air. Wanting away from this place, she tried to fly.

If she had relaxed and allowed the bird body to do what came naturally to it, she would have been fine. But *she* tried to figure it out. Tried to think about flapping wings and air currents and the sensation of the wind over the barbs of her feathers.

And, once again, she fell. It happened so fast. Her little body bounding off of limbs in a graceless plummet to the leaf and twig strewn ground.

Her bird body made a pitiful sound. A twittering moan.

She had broken things. Broken this body. Shattered her chance to escape the elder creatures stalking the night.

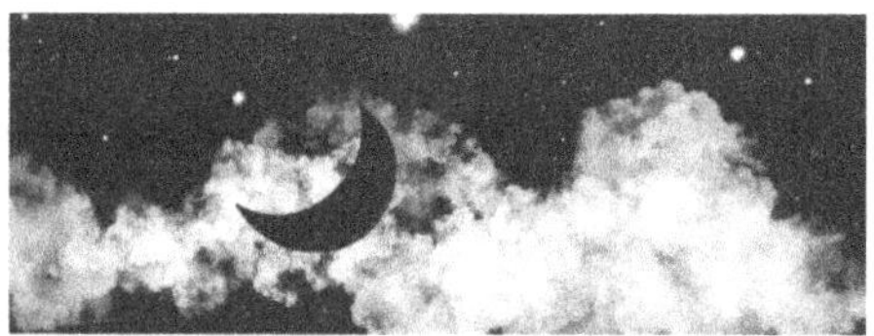

CORA WOKE TO SOBBING MOANS rattling in her chest. She felt pain as she had never felt before. Naked and shattered on the forest floor, she was in her own body. It felt more alien than the bird body had.

To move one finger was to cause pain from the back of her head, up and down her spine, then down the arm to the finger. Bone pieces and snapped sinews and torn flesh ground together or pulled against one another. But move her fingers she did, one at a time. With the speed of the ages, they curled into the foamy surface layer of the forest floor. All the while, the pain swamped through her again and again.

Her mind drifted, seeking escape from the pain. Focused instead on the sensation of spiritual unease. On the whispers. They were saying something was wrong with the world.

Something....

Something....

Memories swam through her mind. Maman. Papa. Elsie. Sun-touched hair and shining eyes and freckled nose—

In Cora's mind, shadows rose and wrapped knife-sharp talons around her young cousin.

Her fingers and toes dug into the old leaves and night dampened earth. Twigs cracked slowly beneath her weight as she crept forward like some twisted eldritch thing, a broken wraith clinging to the ground and driven by a single purpose.

Unable to stop, she pulled herself through forest dirt one agonizing inch at a time. The broken bones in her body grinding as she moved. Dawn came and found her clawing uphill. Her hair had dried in tangles. It was matted now by leaves and twigs and blood and a beetle foraging for breakfast. The beetle crawled in among the black feathers jutting out of the dark, tangled mess.

The feathers smoked.

That smoke drifted down along Cora's body and seeped in through the layers of her skin.

And in the hours she pulled herself along the forest floor, some Power, perhaps the Goddess herself, shielded her from the senses of the hungering, hunting, unseen *bolgken.*

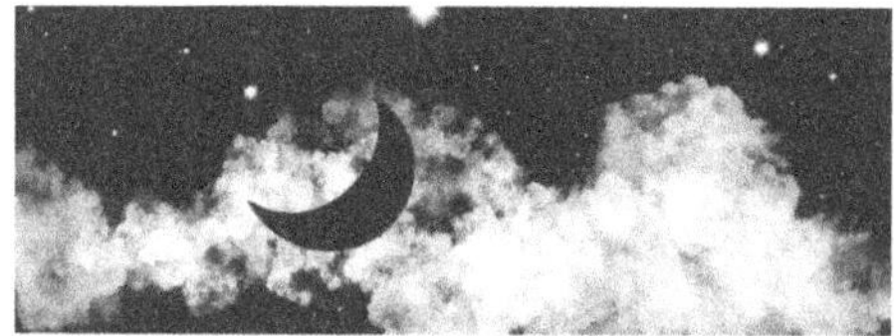

SHE WALKED LIKE A BROKEN doll, arms reaching to catch herself should she fall. Her gait unsteady, leg twisted, hip popped to the side. The intensity of her focus on Elsie drowned out the pain and disorientation. It came upon her in great swirling bursts of the world spinning. Visual whirlwinds. Her sight fracturing into broken shards before putting itself together.

Sounds were different in her ears. A fly buzzing half a field away caught her attention. She turned her head, cocked it, focused in on the fly until it was all she could hear. Then a jay burst up from a nearby bush, screaming a scolding at another bird and Cora screamed, too, as the cries of the jays stabbed into her ears and mind.

Naked, her body misshapen, her mind a fractured thing, she staggered onto the edge of the green, startling the other children who immediately called for the adults.

"Elsie!" Cora called, searching for her cousin among the screaming, scattering children. Her voice emerged as a hoarse croak.

Doors to the houses were flung open as mothers came to see what the commotion was all about. The children pointed to the Cora-wraith, risen to rain vengeance upon the worlds, and the mothers made signs to ward off evil. To ward off the Power. To ward away Bone Crows.

"Elsie!" Cora croaked, stumbling toward Elsie's home beside the very house she, Cora, had been born and raised in. Doors slammed at her approach, but everyone peered through window panes and cracked shutters.

She cried her cousin's name again and the skies darkened. Thunder rolled. Ground lightning crackled over the green grass and wheat-blond fields. Cora's hair lifted into the air, waving as it had under water.

Cora was dimly aware of shouting a long way away and of the men running down the green, farming implements in hand.

She ignored them all and focused on the house where her cousin lived. Movement in the upper window. A small form holding an even smaller one. They created a shadow against the glass. The shadow darkened. Grew larger. The window swung open.

Biting her lower lip, Elsie looked down upon her cousin. Her face was pale, dark circles under her eyes. In her arms, her baby brother wriggled, and the blankets fell away from his upper body.

Cora shrieked a cry of rage as she stared at the babe in her cousin's arm. The creature in the blankets was no longer giggling, pudgy Tam.

The whispers grew loud, a storm thundering through her mind, telling her what she must do. In the darkened sky, thunder rolled. A cluster of violent ground lightning caused the oncoming men to slow their mad rush.

"Cora?" Elsie's voice was barely a whisper. It was sad and weak, the voice of someone who was ill.

"Elsie," Cora croaked a reply. "Throw baby down."

Elsie paled further and pulled back from the window, turning to shield her brother, her eyes wide with shock.

Another cry of rage boiled up Cora's throat and transformed into a caw of challenge. Black smoke writhed round her strange, broken body.

"Away with you, "a voice commanded. It was hoarse and shaky but she recognized it.

"Papa?"

"Be gone, Bone Crow, you are not my Cora."

Cora was surrounded with pitchforks and scythes and hatchets. Young Tom, one summer passed skipping games himself, brandished a branch of wood.

She spun in a slow circle, her naked, twisted body moving in a disjointed, halting dance.

"I am your Cora," she croaked. "You drowned-ed me. But the whispers... the Goddess...."

"Elsie! Come away from that window!" The sound of Aunt Ingra's voice returned Cora's attention to the upper window.

"They are going to hurt her!" the young girl cried as she clutched her brother while still trying to watch the green.

Aunt Ingra wrapped her arms around her daughter. "That isn't Cora," she said, and bodily turned her daughter and son away from the window.

As if these words gave them courage, the field hands came forward, scythes held in front. Young Tom swung his stick. It came inches from Cora's arm. Dark purple flame sprang from Cora and ate the branch which Young Tom dropped, jumping back. The other men shouted and stamped.

Cora lifted her arms toward Elsie's window. Then she was in the air, transforming, painfully. All the healing things inside of her rearranging. Re-snapping. Reforming. Wings beating down. Bone white feathers gleaming. Black smoke whirling. Rising. Flapping toward the window.

Aunt Ingra reached out and slammed the shutter shut just as Cora arrived, and the newly made Bone Crow bounced off. She tumbled down. Her wings fought the fall. Remembering what happened in the forest, she held her breath and allowed her bird body to right itself just above the ground. Then she swooped around and flew to the window.

She flapped her wings furiously and bumped her beak against the shutters Aunt Inga had fastened closed.

She flew to the next window, but it, too, was shut fast. As was the next. Each window failed to grant her access. In some cases, she heard the sound of running feet reaching the window just ahead of her. The thud of the bolt thrust into its hole.

She circled round the house, testing every point of entry, but to no avail. As she sought a way inside, the whispers built in intensity. The Power crackling along her wings in black lightning.

Those on the ground used slingshots to try and bring her down, but she barely noted the thud of stones as they hit the walls around her.

On her third pass around the house, she faltered. The whispers continued to urge her on, demanded she fulfill her part of the bargain, but her stamina weakened. Heart thundering in her chest, she plopped ungracefully on the flower box above the front door. One of the stones caught her on the back of her head and a bright flash of pain burst through her head and lasted for some time.

WHEN THE PAIN CLEARED, SHE was on the grass of the green, in her own body, such as it was, and a gourd cage had been tipped over her. The cage was a basket as tall as a man, woven from threaded mallow into a rounded point at the top. They were called gourd cages, but they served many purposes. Among others, they supported fruit laden plants and formed the shape of the summer bonfires.

The afternoon light had mostly abandoned the sky but the moon was not yet risen. In the dusk, Cora peered through the weave of the gourd cage and watched her aunts and uncles, her older cousins, her family... all the people who had known her since she'd been born. They gathered round her, torches in some hands, firewood in others.

Dirty hair hanging over her eyes, her lips curled back from her teeth, she paced around the small space—not more than three steps from start to finish. She watched her family toss the firewood around the base of her cage.

The torch bearers drew closer.

"Wish you would have stayed drowned," her Papa said. His torch was fat and new, its flame bright. The light glittered off of wetness trickling down his cheeks. "Would have been easier."

She hissed at him, wrapping her fingers through the basket weave and trying to lift the cage. But they had pegged it fast to the ground.

"You would want it this way," her Papa went on. "If you were right in the head. You'd never want to become-" His voice caught and was weaker as he continued. "You love your cousins. You would never try to eat them. This ain't you."

He spoke those words as a final judgement and thrust his torch at the cage. Other torches were touched to it as well, all around her. She smelled the tallow they had been dipped into. Smelled the heat.

Fire caught the woven cage. Crackled. The blaze surrounding her as thoroughly as the cold water had.

When she screamed, the whispers screamed with her, the Power, ...the Goddess, ...the very world screamed along.

The sound of hoofbeats.

The howl of wind.

She looked down on tiny creatures with tiny flames in their hands. They had meant her harm. Now she would destroy them.

The Power demanded it.

She opened her wings and filled the world with her glorious darkness. It was vast, all-powerful. It-

A silver note rang through her glorious dark. A moonbeam through the night. The whispers were pushed back enough to make room for another voice. "Cora? It's– It's me. Elsie. Please, Cora, remember."

The all-consuming darkness receded slowly to be replaced by a somewhat normal night. Cora stood naked in the light of a scattered bonfire, her arm bent awkwardly for balance on legs that were not yet healed. A silver band had been clasped around her upper left arm.

Elsie, still pale and sickly looking, her twisted right foot standing in the grass beside a fat, extinguished torch, had a matching silver band.

"You are Cora. My cousin. And you bloody Pugly's nose if he taunts me."

Cora blinked at her younger cousin. This close, she could see the tendrils of the *bolgken* grub sunk deep into the younger girl's chest and neck. Behind her, Guardian Sardos argued with Aunt Ingra and the other adults while his Witch watched over the cousins. The citizenry of the hamlet gathered between the two but did not approach the Witch.

"Your babe was lost before this night," Sardos said sternly. "Young Cora was attempting to save your daughter."

The roan horse stamped his foot as if in agreement.

Aunt Ingra's face was red, the age lines stark in the torchlight. "I know my own child!"

"Look," the Bone Crow said to Cora, pointing at the babe Aunt Ingra clutched to her shoulder.

Cora hissed quietly at the grub-faced *bolgken* which waved root-arms and drank Elsie's *satha* through the roots sunk deep into her.

When Cora looked at the *bolgken*, it was as if Elsie's eyes were opened. She clutched at her throat, trying to stop her life from being drained. "Please," she whimpered. "I can see with Cora's eyes. That's not my brother."

"Be quiet," Aunt Ingra told her. "Come away with you. Into the house."

"It's eating me, maman."

"Into the house, I said."

Elsie shook her head and touched the band on her arm. "Cora needs me."

"Do what you're told!"

Mother and daughter stared at each other, but Elsie did not back down. "Cora's always watched over me. It's my turn to watch over her. To help her remember who she is."

From somewhere in the crowd, Cora's own maman broke down and sobbed.

"If you think you're doing anything other than taking your medicine and going to bed–"

She was cut off by Sardos who threw his cape over his shoulder, and rested his hand on the pommel of his sword. "The King thanks you for your service, Madam. "

"The king can pucker up his aged, wrinkled lips and kiss my sweet bum," Aunt Ingra snarled. "And so can you. Elsie, come now."

Sardos tilted his head to the side for just a moment before gathering the reins of the roan and vaulting into the saddle. He heeled the roan forward between the girls and the crowd. As he did so, the Bone Witch put her arm around Elsie's shoulders and the two of them were in the saddle of the thorn gray, as if lifted there by the wind.

For a moment, Cora was alone. Then, Guardian Sardos leaned to the side and swept her up. It happened so fast, no one made an attempt to stop them until they were trotting up the cart track.

When they were far enough away from the hamlet that the light of the torches was lost in the trees, they paused. The Witch loosened a blanket from behind her saddle and handed it to Sardos who wrapped it around Cora.

"My name, you know," he said to the girls. "This is Mistress Moirain. I am sorry we did not give you a chance to say goodbye," Sardos said to Elsie. "It is a brave thing you chose to do for your cousin. There are many hard days ahead for you. For both of you."

"What will happen to my family? To... Tam?" Elsie looked no better, but she spoke firmly.

"We will not speak of it here. But we will not forget the peril your family is in, even if they do not believe it."

They rode on, Cora's head resting against Sardos's shoulder much as it had against her father's as he carried her to her death. She felt dazed, as if she'd fallen into a dream from which she could not escape. She didn't want to. The whispers wore her like the *bolkgen* grub wore the baby's face. And she liked it.

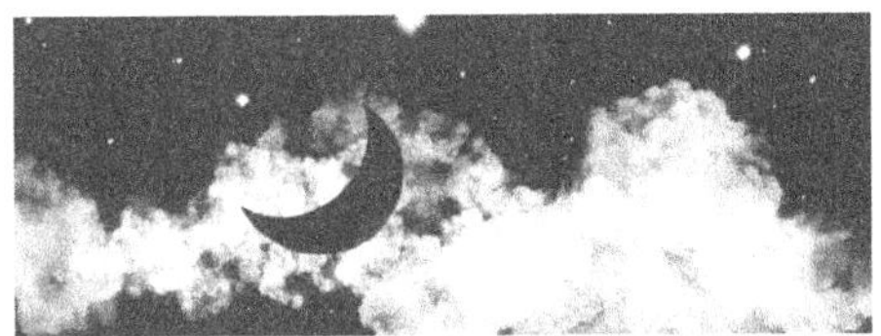

THEY RODE INTO THE NIGHT. When Sardos was convinced they could not be followed, they made camp beneath the light of the moon. The cousins lay beside each other on a saddle blanket, Cora wearing one of the Bone Crow's shifts.

They heard Sardos and his Witch murmuring together, and then silence. Soon, the Guardian found a seat near the girls. He sat with his back to a boulder, keeping watch as the girls lay awake wondering what would happen when the sun rose.

Sometime later, Cora woke when the Bone Witch leaned over them and shook Elsie's shoulder. The younger girl sat up, rubbing her eyes. When she took her hands from her face, she gasped.

On the ground, the *bolgken*-grub that had eaten Elsie's brother and taken his place writhed in anger.

"Touch your band," Sardos told Elsie. "Look hard with your cousin's eyes, so there is no doubt."

Elsie nodded at him and grasped the band on her arm.

Behind Sardos, the male Bone Witch and his Guardian, another thin, young man in a cape and hood, were seeing to their horses. Had they brought the young grub? Cora's mouth watered as she watched the thing wriggle. Her hands curled into claws. The whispers rushed up to fill her ears,

"You're going to be a Guardian, little one," Sardos said to Elsie in a soft voice. "First lesson is–"

Cora didn't hear what the first lesson was. She didn't care. She dove forward, her body transforming. It hurt. Bones breaking. Sinews reshaping. Bone beak stabbed deep into the grubbling.

Thunder rolled.

Her beak shredded flesh and fibrous appendages. She tore the invisible roots from Elsie's neck, then sliced the grub from tip to tip.

She reveled in the savagery. Drank the *satha*. Felt it burn through her like lightning. In that moment, she was one with the Goddess.

The whispers danced with glee. The Power filled her. She'd never wanted this but perhaps the Goddess had always known she was a Little Crow at heart. She'd bloodied noses to stand up for Elsie and she'd eat all the grubbling children in the world if it kept the others safe.

The whispers loved her and promised her the darkness and the Power.

She opened her beak and sang of her own glory. Sent her challenge into the world. Offered her thanks for the gift of being a Bone Crow.

The Goddess smiled, and the moon shone on Cora's bone white face and black, magic wings.

A lover of night swimming and firefly catching, Karlie Stites would be happy with any kind of wings that would allow her to fly.

Inspired by her love of Norse mythology and a piece of art created by her sister, she tells us the story of a strong Valkyrie discovering her true strength, as often happens, through pain and loss

DAWN OF VENGEANCE

Karli Stites

I KNOW SOMETHING'S WRONG WHEN I hear the call. The haunting melody of the fighting horn. I've only heard the sound a handful of times, but this time feels different.

The air is heavy with panic. When the horn stops, my ears prick and the blood drains from my face because I hear *screaming*. Cries of terror from the children. Warrior roars from those of fighting age. I want to cover my ears—my enhanced hearing makes the thunderous noise painful. But I can't because I need to know what's happening.

"Valeria!" My twin sister's voice calls to me from across our house, but I barely hear her over the sound of clashing swords, screaming, and crying.

I look at the rumpled blankets on my bed, trying to recall the last thing I did before I went to sleep, but come up blank.

"Honor!" I yell. My voice is lined with confusion, but I'm too scared to hide it.

My twin runs into the room we share dressed ready for battle. We're identical down to the very freckle, except for one glaring difference: our eyes. Mine are pure violet, and hers the clear blue of the ocean.

Her armor is black as night, like our hair. The titanium-diamond alloy wraps around her body like a second skin, protecting her from any enemies that seek to destroy us. Her ocean-blue eyes are open wide, and they match the straps that crisscross her body, securing her weapons. In one hand, she holds a glowing white sword. It burns with the power granted to us by the Goddess of Night, Nótt. Strapped to her other arm is her signature weapon—a crossbow—and she carries sheaths of glowing knives on each thigh. Her golden wings are extended behind her, rising up as if to join her in battle.

She looks ready to fight.

"Honor, what's going on?" I grab her hand. "I heard the call..."

"It's chaos. A bloodbath. Some are already dead. Some are just *gone.* "

"What?" I whisper. My voice is hoarse. My world spins on its axis as everything I know to be true changes in a moment.

"We need to go," she urges. "We need to fight."

I look at her incredulously. "We can't! We're not allowed." Valkyrie aren't blooded into the Warriors until fifteen, and we still have two months to go.

Honor gets a steely glint in her eye, showing me why she's the brave one who likes to bend the rules. "Now's not the time to follow tradition, Valeria. We need to fight for our family. For our home. We can't stand back this time. They *need us.*"

My back straightens. I may be a rule follower, threatened by the harsh words of our mother to behave in a manner befitting the Valkyrie, but I'm not a coward. I nod as I meet her eyes, determination filling my body and strengthening my spirit.

"There's my girl." Honor smiles. "Get dressed."

I sprint to my wardrobe, changing in record time. My armor is identical to hers, but my straps mirror my eye color. I hold my glowing sword in my right hand and my weapon of choice—a glowing spear that returns to me after I throw it—in my left. I also have extra knives strapped to my arms and ankles because *you can never have too many knives.* Two minutes later, I'm ready.

I take a deep breath, meet my sister's eyes, and nod. "Let's go."

She looks me over from head to toe and smirks. "Lookin' good, sis."

I roll my eyes. "We look the same."

"Exactly."

I smile. Honor always knows how to lighten the mood. For a second, I almost forget our clan is dying. My heart clenches in my chest. I meet her eyes one last time before we walk out the door and grab her hand.

"Honor, wait." She raises an eyebrow. "I love you."

"Valeria, relax. It's going to be fine. Don't worry." She smirks again and winks. "Nothing can take me down."

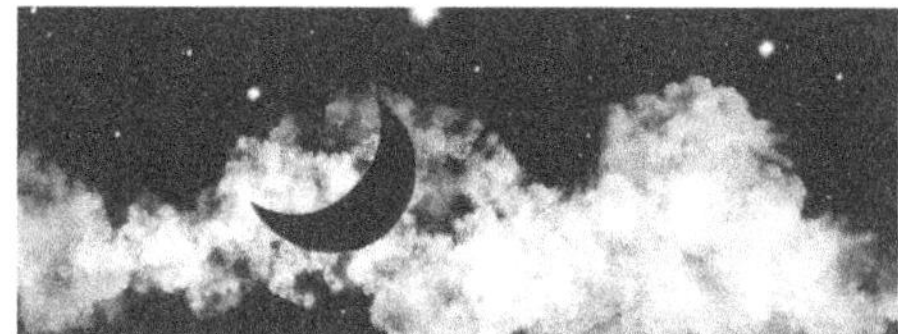

ASH COATS MY TONGUE. BLOOD coats my skin. And pain coats my mind.

Nothing will be the same.

Nothing can take me down. Nothing can take me down. Nothing. Can. Take. Me. Down. Honor's words play on repeat in my mind. The words she'd spoken to me before everything changed. My twin. She's gone. Taken. Captured by an unknown enemy that hunted us, seeking to claim what wasn't theirs.

My family, my clan, and everything I've ever known. All gone in the blink of an eye.

I have nothing left.

Bodies litter the ground. I remember hearing the intruders scream that we *weren't to be harmed*, but I know my clan and they'd rather die than go down without a fight. Still, some bodies were missing from the carnage, so I know they'd managed to capture some of us after all. My beloved twin included.

My mother wasn't as lucky. Or maybe she was. I'm not yet sure which fate is worse.

During the invasion, the intruders set fire to many of our buildings, trying to smoke us out. Then, they attacked. Viciously and without mercy. At the end of the battle, I searched through our decimated city and found forty-four bodies. Forty-four fallen sisters. Forty-four beautiful Valkyrie that will never again see the light of day. Never open their eyes again.

My only hope lay with the missing. Five of them. I know they're still alive because I feel it in my bones. In my blood. In my soul.

I'll get them back.

Honor. Raelin. Alessia. Aurora. Xera.

We'll be together again. And the intruders will pay for their crimes. They'll regret the day they messed with the Moonbound Valkyrie. My heart hardens as my vow settles in my chest.

I fall to my knees and pray.

"Goddess of the Night, I pray to thee of the Moonbound Valkyrie." I turn my face up to the moon, the light bathing me in an ethereal glow. "Goddess, grant me strength when I have little. Grant me the power to exact justice and avenge my clan for the wrongs exacted upon us this Darkest Night."

My eyes harden with resolve. "For I was Valeria of the Moonbound, but I am Vengeance."

Her voice comes with the wind. A sweet melody edged with temptation and the sense of something wicked.

Daughter, I hear your prayer.

I startle. "Nótt?"

Yes, Daughter. Your pain calls to me. Your sweet vengeance sits heavy on my heart. I wish to help. These intruders have taken from me. You'll bleed them dry with my blessing.

"Yes, Goddess."

I will grant you the strength to carry on. The sacrifice will be great, should you choose to accept.

"I accept," I say without a moment of hesitation. "I'll bleed from a thousand cuts and die a thousand deaths before I let the invaders get away with this."

I feel her pleasure at my response. *You'll find much of your blood will spill before this is over.*

"A worthy sacrifice."

You are strong. Prepare yourself. Your new life begins tonight. I wish you well, my Daughter of Night.

I feel her presence leave. A moment later, the pain begins. Blinding pain. Like nothing I've ever felt before. I bow my head and scream. Scream and scream and scream. They echo in the silence, bouncing off the ruined buildings that lay in cinders around me.

I feel my feathers—my beautiful golden feathers—plucked from my back as if with invisible fingers. Phantom hands that aren't gentle. They lay in tatters at my feet. I cry as they fall. The pain is unbearable.

My eyes burn. My back burns. My skin burns.

And then it stops.

And I feel…changed. Utterly, irrevocably changed.

I run to the nearest house. The door is open, so I burst in with no resistance. I come to a stop inside the door when I see my reflection in the hallway mirror.

My mouth drops open. "Oh, my goddess."

I look like a different person. I feel a sharp pain in my chest as I think of Honor, my twin who I barely resemble anymore.

My endlessly long hair, tied back into two braids, has gone completely white. As white as snow. My skin has a pearlescent sheen, reminiscent of the moon. My violet eyes are brighter, glowing with power. And my beautiful golden wings are as black as night. Sharp like knives. I touch one and my finger instantly bleeds.

I'm now a weapon forged by the Goddess of Night.

I sigh in relief. I can work with this. This is strength. This will save my clan. Save my sister.

Suddenly, I feel my wings retract and I panic. *My wings!* I turn around, desperate to find them, clawing at my back, and find a sigil tattooed across my flesh. From the bottom of my hairline to the base of my spine and extending across my entire back, where my wings used to be, is a pair of solid black wings. Inked right on my skin.

I stop moving and stare. I've never seen *anything* like it before.

You can call on them when you need them.

"How?" I ask my goddess.

You'll know, she replies cryptically.

I nod in determination, ready to face my new life.

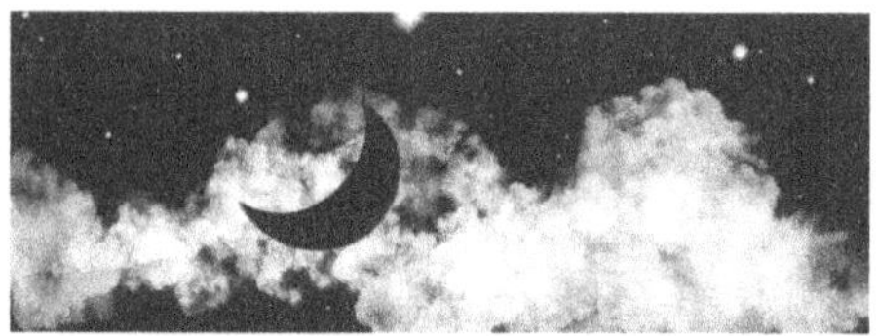

Six Years Later

WHERE ARE THEY?" I ASK, holding a glowing knife up to my captive's throat. He spits blood at my feet, and I curl my lip in disgust. I nick his skin with my blade and his eyes flare in panic.

"I'll never tell you. They'll kill me."

"*I'll* kill you," I say coldly.

He laughs manically. "You can't do shit to me, little girl. You're nothing. You'll never be able to go up against *them.*"

I sigh. It's the same old story. None of the men I've found and interrogated have spilled any information about the missing Valkyrie. *Who the Hel were they taken by that has them so scared?*

Whoever they are, I'm not worried. I've spent the last six years honing my body to perfection. I'm a warrior, a weapon, and I'm made for violence. I'm no longer the scared twin sister of Honor. I'm a Valkyrie.

I grin wickedly at my captive and I see his face shift from confident to uneasy. I'm used to being underestimated. In fact, I think it's one of my favorite parts of my transformation. The ethereal appearance makes me look delicate and my hidden wings help me stay incognito.

"I'm glad you said that," I say to him. I see the question in his eyes, but I don't wait for him to ask. "It only makes it that much sweeter."

"What—"

"Ég hefna mín," I whisper, cutting him off. He screams when my wings burst from my back, the beautiful sigil shifting into black knives of destruction and power. They rip out of my skin, the pain blinding, but not as much as that first night. The tips drip with the blood of my sacrifice.

I bow my head in reverence. "May the Goddess accept my sacrifice."

When I lift my head, my captive looks terrified. His screams have died down, but his eyes are wide, and his hands clench tightly into fists.

"What the hell are you?" He whispers. I don't think he means for me to hear.

I laugh. "Valkyrie."

He shakes his head. "You're no Valkyrie."

I shrug. "I'm blessed by the Goddess." His eyes widen further, and they look comically large in his pinched face. I sigh, sick of playing this game.

Calling on my Goddess-blessed powers, I clench my back. One of the knives grows hot, glows bright white, and shoots right out of my back, landing perfectly in my hand. I smirk when the man tied to the chair in front of me pisses himself.

"I'll give you one last chance to tell me what I want to know before I slit your throat."

"I don't know anything!" He yells. I walk forward, holding the knife up threateningly.

He slumps over in the chair. "Fine! Yes, I was there that night, but I'm just paid muscle. I helped gather up the Valkyrie. That's all."

I grit my teeth. "You did more than *gather up* the Valkyrie." I lean forward, getting close to his face. My violet eyes burn with my rage and the glow intensifies until I see it reflected in his gaze. "Forty-four died that night."

He gulps. "That wasn't supposed to happen! They fought back. Things just got out of hand... We only ended up getting five."

I seethe. "I know exactly how many Valkyrie you got." I resist the urge to stab him. I need more information.

"Where are they?" I grit out through clenched teeth.

"I don't know. They didn't take us back where they came from. They just paid us and left."

"Who are they?"

"I don't know!"

"Well then, I guess there's no reason for me to keep you alive then, is there?"

"Wait!" he yells. "Wait, I might know something else. There's another we were supposed to capture... A Berserker living on his own. He fought us off. He might know more. I think they've tried to go after him before."

I purse my lips. "Do you have a name?"

"No, but he wasn't too far away from where your clan lived. I'm sure you won't have too much trouble finding him. He's certainly made a name for himself. A lone Berserker? It wasn't hard to find him the first time. He doesn't take too kindly to visitors though."

"Okay." I nod. "Thank you. That's good information."

He sighs in relief.

I raise an eyebrow. "I don't know why you're relieved. I'm still going to kill you."

"Bu—but I helped you!" he sputters.

"You killed my family," I point out. "Say hello to your friends in Helheim."

I stab him in the heart, twist the knife, and then slit his throat for good measure. The light leaves his eyes, but I feel nothing. Another day, another death. But *finally*, I'm one step closer to finding my sister and the rest of my clan. Only five of us left.

I'll destroy worlds to get them back. And maybe, I just might end up doing that by the time this is all over. I only hope I don't destroy myself, and my soul in the process.

WHEN I WALK IN THE bar, all eyes turn towards me. After six years, I'm used to it. No one knows what to make of a woman dressed like a Valkyrie that looks like me—especially one with no wings. I give them all a sharp smile; all teeth and no sweetness. I like to keep them guessing.

I don't tend to broadcast my status of Goddess-blessed. Usually, the only ones who know my secret are about to meet their death at the end of my blade. Or my crossbow. I took up the weapon after losing Honor. When I get her back, I'm going to show her all the tricks I've learned over the years. And it is a *when*, not an *if*. I refuse to believe another alternative.

A few men give me lingering stares and I narrow my eyes. I feel them flash with power, the violet glow brightening and causing most of my admirers to gulp and look away. I don't trust men. Especially after my home was invaded by them and they stole my family from me, changing my life forever. No. I don't trust men. I'll never trust another man again.

But I'm here for a reason. And that reason is to find a lone Berserker. Name unknown. Location unknown. I figure Hel's Gate is as good a place as any to meet some *questionable* characters who might have information on where I can find him. A Berserker. I huff. I can't believe I'm even entertaining the idea of working with one. They're insane. Or so I've heard. I haven't actually met one before.

I walk up to the bar and take a seat directly in front of the bartender. I look him up and down. Wolf shifter. One of Fenrir's offspring. I groan because he can probably smell what I am. He looks at me and raises an eyebrow when he sees the expression on my face.

Instead of speaking—likely calling out my Valkyrie status for everyone to hear—he simply nods and pushes over a drink. I take a sip and smile in thanks. A *small* smile because I still don't trust men and I don't want him getting any ideas.

He sees me eye him with suspicion and laughs. "Relax, gorgeous. Not everyone is out to get you."

I resist the urge to punch him for the pet name, because he's a wolf and they're all like that. I shake my head instead.

"That's not been my experience."

"That's sad, love," he says. And he really does look sad. It's weird. My life has been cold, dark, and lonely for so long, I'm not used to sympathy.

"I get by just fine on my own," I mutter.

He nods. "I'm sure you do. But don't you ever get lonely?"

Yes. "No."

I cut him off before he can respond to my obvious lie. "So, I'm looking for someone."

He smirks. "Aren't we all?"

I glare. "This is business."

He holds up both hands. "Fine, fine. Who is it?"

I look around, wishing we weren't surrounded for this conversation, but as nice as he seems, I still don't trust him enough to be alone with him. Out of the corner of my eye, I spy someone listening to us. I'd call him out for it, but I'm curious, so I decide to wait him out. Maybe he'll know something about my mysterious Berserker. Or maybe he's responsible for the death of my family and he'll have to die. Either way works for me.

He's in the shadows, so I can't make out what he looks like. Can't tell if he's one of the men who ravaged my city that night. I grit my teeth. I'll wait. But only so long before my patience wears thin.

"He's…" I trail off with a grimace. "A Berserker."

The bartender's mouth drops open, but he quickly covers his surprise. I see my shadow stiffen a little in the corner of the bar. *Jackpot.*

"A Berserker, huh?" The bartender scratches the scruff on his face. "I've heard a few whispers, but never seen anything around these parts. A rogue?"

"Yes."

"They're dangerous, doll," he warns.

"So am I."

He nods slowly. "Yeah, I see that."

I stand up, pushing back from my chair and draining the rest of my drink in one gulp. "Thanks for the drink."

"Daemon," he supplies, even though I didn't ask.

"Thanks, Daemon. It's been…fun."

He laughs and winks. "No problem, gorgeous. I'll see you around."

I snort. "Not likely."

Then, I turn around and make my way across the bar, my unbound white hair brushing my thighs and swishing around my body as I walk. I'm armed to the teeth as usual, and I hope it discourages anyone from coming after me. Although, I'm confident my shadow—the mysterious stranger who watched me in the bar—will follow. In fact, I'm counting on it. I know he has the information I need. And I'm ready to fight for it. Whatever it takes.

I slip out the door and to the side of the building, leaning against the cool brick. I wait.

Not a minute passes before he comes for me.

I grab him by his cloak—a ridiculous outfit for fighting—and throw him up against the wall. He's bigger than me, but he's not expecting it. He doesn't fight my hold. I'm confused by his complacency, but I don't loosen my arm. My eyes widen when I get a good look at him. Almost two full heads taller than me, black hair, light blue eyes, and utterly recognizable grey skin. I know his skin is impenetrable. He'd be a tough adversary. A worthy opponent.

"Gargoyle," I spit out. "Why are you following me?"

I know instantly he wasn't there that night, but I don't let him go. I still don't know his intentions. Gargoyles may be honorable protectors, but he's still a man.

"I heard you inside," he says in a gruff voice. "Why are you looking for the Berserker?"

My eyes narrow on his. "Why? Do you know him?"

He sighs. "No one *knows* him. But I've seen him fight. He's a savage. Not someone you want to meet."

I tighten my arm on his neck. "You know, *Shadow*, I'm getting really sick and tired of people telling me what I can and can't do."

"I'm just saying it's not safe for you."

"You don't *know me*," I grit out. I push back from him, letting him go. He obviously thinks he's some sort of white knight, trying to save me. A helpless damsel in distress. I roll my eyes. Gargoyles. "No one knows me. No one knows what I'm capable of.

He holds his hands up. "Listen, Killer, I didn't mean to offend you. I'm only trying to help."

"I don't need your help," I say.

Then I speak my truth under my breath and my wings extend from my back, glorious in their viciousness. Beautiful in their righteousness. Deadly in their vengeance.

"Valkyrie," he breathes reverently.

I raise an eyebrow, dumbfounded. That's...not what I expected.

"Uhm," I stammer unintelligently.

He laughs joyfully. "I haven't seen your kind in millennia. I have to admit, the legends don't do you justice." I scowl. "You're a little feistier than I expected. More bloodthirsty."

I roll my eyes. "Well, that's bound to happen when your entire clan is murdered."

His mouth drops open and my shoulders slump in defeat. He was my last lead to find my family.

Besides the Berserker, a little voice whispers in the back of my head. I straighten. Right. Besides the psycho murdering machine. Looks like I'm going hunting.

The Gargoyle reaches towards me and I narrow my eyes, warning him away before he makes contact. He backs up. Smart man.

"I'm sorry about your family," he says. He sounds genuine. I swallow, my heart clenching in my chest as the pain threatens to overwhelm me.

"Thanks."

We stare at each other for a minute in silence. When he doesn't say anything else, I retract my wings and decide to make my exit.

"Well, Shadow, I better be going. I have a Berserker to find."

I move to leave, but he catches my hand. His skin is cold, and it feels weird. I haven't touched another living being in six years apart from in battle, blood, and violence. I startle and jump back.

"Wait, don't leave."

I roll my eyes. "I have to go. I have a Berserker to catch and interrogate. He has information I need."

"Like what?"

I don't answer. He sighs, frustrated with my silence. "Let me come with you."

"No," I reply immediately. "I work alone."

"Come on, Killer. I can help. I'm telling you; this guy is crazy. And I've never fought beside a Valkyrie. I'm intrigued. You'd be doing me a favor."

I see what he's doing, and I'm not falling for it. "I don't need help."

"I'm a pilot. I have a ship. I'll take you anywhere you want to go."

I perk up. Now *that's* an offer I can't refuse.

"You have a deal."

He grins. "Let's go then. Your chariot awaits."

"You got a name, Shadow?"

"Yeah," he nods. "Valor."

Valor. *Seriously?* I grimace. It suits him. But... Valor and Valeria? We sound like a twisted team of vigilantes.

He looks at me. "How about you, Valkyrie?"

"Call me V."

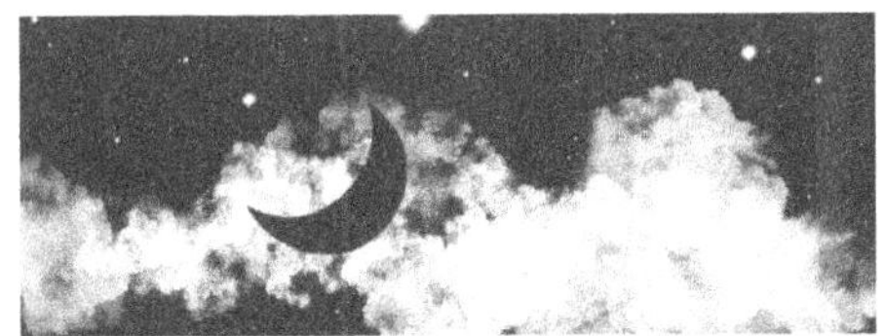

SO, V, WHERE ARE WE headed?" Valor asks me once we get inside his ship.

I look at him in his captain's seat and consider his question. He's taken off the cloak, so his wings are on display. I examine them, cataloguing their strengths and weaknesses in the blink of an eye. They're grey, the same color as his skin, and an interesting mix of webbed flesh. I know they can harden to stone at his will. *Interesting.* I dart my eyes away before he notices me staring.

"Where it all began." I pause. "My home."

He nods, waiting for me to explain. "I'll have to direct you there. The location isn't broadcasted. We were pretty secretive about it. I still don't know how they found us."

"Okay, sounds good. I can do that. Tell me where to go, then." He eyes me. "It's on this planet, right?"

"What?" He *must* be joking. I ignore him, pretending I didn't hear because I'm *confused as Hel* and I don't want to think about what his question could mean for my sister and the rest of my missing clan. My heart races so I quickly change the subject to calm myself.

"My home isn't too far from here. Maybe a day's flight." I frown. "At least on my old wings..."

He perks up and my accidental admission. "Old wings?"

I shoot him a glare. I'm obviously not responding to that.

"Got it," he laughs. "The wings are off limits."

I roll my eyes. "Yes. Now pay attention."

A couple hours later, we're breaking through the trees and coming to a halt in front of my city: the city of the Moonbound Valkyrie. Once a sight to behold. Now, nothing but ash and abandoned buildings left to rot. This city will never be the glory it once was. We'll never be able to rebuild. We were once fifty strong. But those days are gone. They're nothing but a memory.

"Wow," Valor comments. "I can't believe I'm seeing this. It's surreal."

"Surprised, Shadow?"

He sighs, exasperated. "I have a name and you know it. You asked for it, after all."

"Shadow suits you better," I smirk. "*After all,* you were skulking about in the shadows, stalking me."

"I wasn't *skulking about.* I was hiding my wings. Hel's Gate isn't really the place for a Gargoyle to hang out. And I wasn't stalking you. I was just watching out for you."

I purse my lips. "Why were you at Hel's Gate anyway?"

He smiles. "I'll tell you my secrets when you tell me yours, *V.*"

I hear the taunt in his voice, and I roll my eyes. I know he's not entirely pleased I refuse to tell him my real name, but I can't bring myself to trust him. He's a man, and I don't trust men. It's my one hard and fast rule. I would have given him the nickname Honor used to call me, Val, but that's even worse. *Valor and Val.* Goddess help me.

"Touché, *Valor.*" I smirk. His smile drops and he frowns a little. I feel kind of bad for hurting his feelings, so I quickly change the subject. Again.

"Let's touch down here. I want to survey the area first. My information says the Berserker lives somewhere close by here. He was supposed to be captured along with the rest of my clan, but he escaped. I want to check out the area where the main fight took place, examine where the ship was, and see if I can find any other clues. If he was ever here, hopefully, I'll catch a trail. If not, we'll fan out from here and search the area."

Valor nods. "Okay, will do, Boss." He pauses. "When did this battle take place? It looks like it wasn't too long ago."

"My city was decimated by men and my family stolen from me on the Darkest Night. Six years ago."

"I see," he says. I look at him and he seems to have come to some conclusion about me. I narrow my eyes, unsure how I feel about that. *What does he think he knows about me?*

"Let's go, Shadow."

"Aye, Boss." He smirks. I roll my eyes.

He's very...playful. I don't know how I feel about it. It's not making me uncomfortable, but I'm not used to being around someone who's so *light*. He reminds me of Honor. She was like that, in a way. Always the light in my life. It makes me feels squirmy—itchy and hot—that he's so *pleasant* to be around. Like he's trying to worm his way under my skin. It should be impossible because *I don't trust men,* but Valor has a special quality that makes him impossible to deny.

Valor touches down and I stand up, ready to go. As soon as he opens the doors to his ship, I'm walking down the platform and escaping into the daylight. I breathe in the crisp mountain air once my feet touch the soil. It tastes like home.

The last time I was here, I still felt the ash on my tongue. So much I almost choked on it. Now if I close my eyes, I can pretend it didn't happen.

I don't do that, though. I need to remember. The pain keeps me going. It's the only thing keeping me alive at this point.

"Stay close," I call out over my shoulder as I start to walk away.

I go through every nook and cranny of the city meticulously. It takes hours and hours, but I find nothing. I avoid the main battlefield. I avoid going into homes. But every other street, alley, and public place is fair game. There's nothing. My Shadow follows my every move, going over everything I look at to make sure I don't miss anything.

I want to scream in frustration. My intentions must show on my face because Valor takes a few steps forward and sidles up to my side.

"Hey, Killer. What's going on?"

I grit my teeth. "There's nothing here. Absolutely no evidence or clues as to who they were or where the Berserker might be."

He nods slowly. "Okay, well, we still have one more place to look, yeah?"

"Yes," I admit. "But maybe we can make one more stop first?"

Valor can tell I'm procrastinating, but he smiles instead of calling me out on it. I appreciate his kindness. "Lead the way, Valkyrie."

It takes five minutes to walk to my house. Or the house I shared with my mother and my sister. It's one of the few that remain standing. We lived on the outskirts of the city where the damage was less extensive.

"This was my house," I say. "I just want to take a quick look inside."

"Of course. I'll stay out here."

"Wait." I grab his hand. "Will you come inside?"

I don't know why I ask. I'm supposed to be strong. Forged by the Goddess to be her weapon. But I can't stomach the idea of walking into my childhood home alone. The home I shared with my family. I can't stand the idea of walking into the room I shared with my twin sister. My sister who's missing. She's been gone for six years and I still haven't found her. I've *failed her.* And it eats me up inside every day of my life.

He nods and follows me without a word. I appreciate the silence. I appreciate a lot of things about him. He's not so bad to have around. For a man, that is. It's almost nice...having a friend.

A friend. Huh. I guess that's what he is.

We walk inside the door and I immediately turn right. I go straight to my old room. I stop in the middle. It's exactly the way I left it.

My side of the room is meticulously clean. My white sheets are tucked in tightly to the mattress, an extra blanket folded neatly at the end of my bed. There are two lines of weapons hanging on the walls in even lines. An organized bookshelf is in the corner, sorted by subject and then author. My wardrobe is closed, but everything would be perfectly tidy if I opened it. Color-coded. Although almost everything on my side is in shades of white, black, and grey.

The other side of the room is the exact opposite. It looks like a color wheel threw up. Honor's sheets are vibrant blue, falling off the mattress. She has an electric purple blanket hanging off one side. Her clothes are haphazardly thrown all over the place, her weapons hanging in seemingly random patterns.

My grief overwhelms me for a moment as I stare at the differences in our personalities. Honor was so free. She was everything to me. And now she's gone.

I see the question in Valor's eyes. I sigh, deciding he deserves an answer since I dragged him inside as my emotional buffer.

"My sister. Twin sister. Honor." I swallow. "This was our room."

"Let me guess," he says pointing to the crazy, unorganized side. "Yours?"

I raise an eyebrow and we both laugh. The mood shifts and I feel lighter. A little less like I'm drowning. I shoot him a grateful smile.

"Honor was always the wild one. Sometimes I think she purposefully did things to drive me crazy."

He laughs. "Why do I feel like it didn't take much to drive you crazy?"

I huff. I mean...he's not wrong. I've always liked things a certain way. I felt like I needed to be the perfect Valkyrie. But despite my best efforts over the past six years, I'm still not good enough. I still can't find Honor.

Valor walks around the room and comes to an abrupt stop when he sees an old picture of Honor and me hanging on the wall. I see the questions in his eyes. I look different: my hair, my skin, my wings, my eyes. I was always beautiful, sure, but I've been transformed into an ethereal being. I was always strong, yes, but I've been forged into a weapon. I was always a Valkyrie, of course, but I've been reborn into something new.

I look away. I'm not ready to divulge all my secrets. Maybe I'll tell him in the future. Maybe I'll never tell him my full story. Can I trust him? Hours ago, the answer to that question was a resounding *no.* But now, things are different. I'm starting to feel like we're friends. I'm starting to think he might actually care. It's a dangerous thought. I don't need ties holding me back. I have a mission to carry out.

"Let's go to the battlefield," I say.

We leave in silence. It takes ten minutes to get to the site of carnage. I take a deep breath when the open field comes into view. It pains me to look at, but I force myself to stare. I *need* to look.

I see the horror in Valor's eyes as he surveys the field. He knew my family was murdered. Slaughtered. But I doubt he expected the scattered burnt remains of the once-great Valkyrie.

"I haven't been back since the Darkest Night. I lost forty-nine of my clan: forty-four dead and five still missing." I pause. "I never found Honor's body."

Valor looks at me with sympathy in his eyes, letting me speak. I've never told this story, except in rage as I interrogated my enemies, draining them of their blood the same way they'd done to my sisters. No mercy. No regrets. Exactly the way my Goddess expected me to.

"I fought that night. I wasn't supposed to. Honor and I weren't blooded yet. Not full Valkyrie warriors." His eyes go wide with understanding. "But she wanted to fight. She knew we had to fight. And I agreed. But I was always scared of breaking the rules. I lived by them. I liked rules and order. I wanted to be the perfect Valkyrie."

I snort in disgust. "Funny how things turn out, right?"

"I don't think so," he starts slowly. "I think you're pretty great."

I laugh without humor. "You don't know me, Shadow. I've done things a Valkyrie would never do. I can't come back from them. I've chosen my path. There's no going back for me."

“Maybe you’re not as far in the dark as you think you are.”

“Yeah, maybe,” I say. But I don’t believe it.

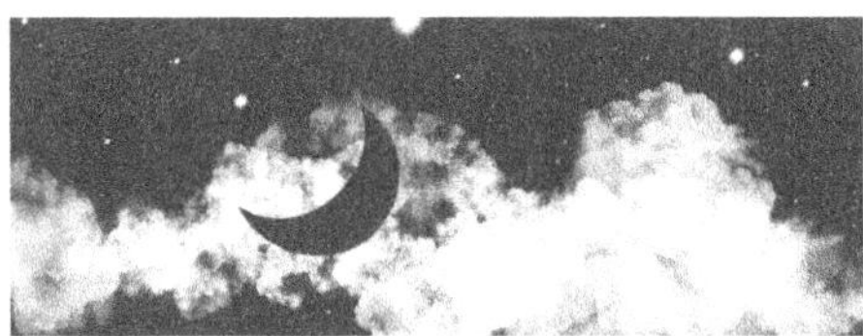

A FEW HOURS LATER, WE’VE searched the entire battlefield and found nothing. I had to stop a few times to ward off flashbacks, but for the most part, we worked in companionable silence.

I avoid going to the place where I made my vow. It’s too personal. Like If I allow Valor to see it, he’ll see every part of me, laid bare at my most vulnerable. I can’t allow that. Not ever again. Especially not with him. He has a way about him. He sees too much. I worry what he might uncover about me.

I might have let my mind—or my eyes—wander for too long, though, because I hear Valor call out and I know he’s found it. The spot where everything’s changed. I run, but it’s too late. He’s seen it all.

“What—”

“Get away from there!” I yell.

“V, what is this?”

He refuses to move. I know why; I know what he sees. My beautiful golden feathers still lay in tatters on the ground, in the same place where they were ripped from my back six years ago. Surrounding them, burned into the ground, is the sigil tattooed on my back. There are drops of blood soaked into the earth, the physical evidence of my sacrifice. Claw marks on the ground from where I begged and screamed from the pain. It's my own little battlefield.

"It's nothing," I say.

Valor grabs my hand. "Who did this to you?" His voice is pained. "V, it looks like you were *tortured*."

I yank my hand back. "I wasn't. It was a blessing. I'm Goddess-blessed. I prayed for strength, and she gave it to me. I'm a weapon. I was made like this for a *reason. I wanted this*."

Valor looks sad. He doesn't believe me. I want to scream that I don't need his pity or his judgment. I'm *strong*. Powerful.

"As entertaining as this is, I'm going to have to interrupt."

I whip around to face the newcomer and my mouth drops open when I come face-to-face with the object of my search.

"Berserker."

"Valkyrie," he replies. "I hear you've been looking for me?"

I look him over, surprised to find he looks nothing like I expected. His appearance is almost angelic. He looks like a golden god. A mountain of a man—even taller than Valor—with golden skin and golden blonde hair. He's heavily muscled and I know they aren't just for show. But it's his eyes that give him away. Pure black. The eyes of a Berserker. There's no light in him. Only darkness.

"I have," I reply. No use denying it. "How'd you find me?"

He laughs darkly. "Wasn't very hard. You were asking around about me pretty loudly at Hel's Gate. There aren't many females who look like you. Word gets around." He shrugs. "Even for an outcast like me."

"Hm," I say. "I got the impression no one liked you."

The Berserker barks out a laugh. This time he actually sounds amused. "I like you, Valkyrie."

"The feeling isn't mutual."

"Ouch," he says as he laughs, holding a hand to his chest. I narrow my eyes.

Why is he joking around so much? "Shouldn't you be trying to kill me?"

Valor, content until now to watch me take the lead, moves forward, his eyes bugging out of his head. I hold him back. The Berserker laughs again.

"Do you *want* me to kill you?"

"Not particularly," I answer.

"Great! I'm not in the killing mood anyway."

I give him a dry mood. "Goody. I'm so relieved."

He's full-on chuckling now. "Yes, I definitely like you."

"Like I said, Berserker, I *don't* like you."

"Why not? I think we can be friends." He looks at me with a fake pout. Somehow, he doesn't look ridiculous. He still manages to seem dangerous.

"Why?" I ask, suspicious of his intentions.

"I think we have similar goals," he says simply. "The enemy of my enemy is my friend."

"Fine," I sigh. "I'll hear you out. What's your story, Berserker?"

"First off, my name isn't Berserker." He smirks. "It's Kian."

"Okay." I groan. "Tell me your story, *Kian*."

He grins, obviously liking the sound of his name on my lips. I roll my eyes. This Berserker—Kian—is trouble.

"Well, if I'm going to tell you my life story, I think you should tell me something, too, Valkyrie."

I get an uneasy feeling in my gut. I know what he's going to ask, and I don't want to tell him. I don't want to give that piece of me away. He smiles evilly, his eyes lighting up with pleasure.

"Tell me your name," he purrs.

"No." It's a ridiculous refusal at this point. He could easily figure it out now that we're in my home city, but I know he won't accept it unless he hears it from me.

Valor's eyes are wide as he looks back and forth between us, sizing up the Berserker, assessing his strengths and weaknesses. I see the moment he realizes he can't take him on. He knows I don't want to give up my name. He hasn't pushed for it since I said no the first time.

Kian's eyes flash and he licks his lips. He looks lethal, excited by the prospect of getting a piece of my soul. "No name, no deal."

"Seriously?" I groan in frustration. "Why do you care about my name?"

He shrugs. "I have my reasons."

"Fine," I spit out. "It's Valeria."

His black eyes light up. "Valeria of the Moonbound Valkyrie. It's a pleasure to make your acquaintance."

I glare and he laughs.

"Alright, I'll tell you what you want to know."

I wait.

"They started coming after me about five years ago. Don't ask me who they are because I have no idea. What I *do* know is that they're ruthless. And determined. I can't say why they want me either. But I've fought like Hel to get away from them. They almost got me last time when they captured your Valkyrie friends." He pauses. "I'm sorry about that, by the way. They were vicious in their fury, but they didn't stand a chance. They ended up being overpowered. I tried to help, but there was only so much I could do."

I nod. I'm surprised he tried to help. It's more than I expected of him, anyway.

"I ended up escaping," he continues. "They drugged your friends and brought them inside their ship."

"Did you see where they went?" I ask desperately.

"That's the weird thing…" He frowns. "I swear, they *flew into space.*"

My mouth drops open in stunned surprise. I immediately glance at Valor, remembering his comment from earlier, and he looks *guilty.* I walk up to him and grab his collar, dragging him towards me.

"Explain," I grit out. "Now."

"V, I didn't know," he pleads. "I had *no idea* it was them."

Kian's black eyes flash dangerously red. "What is he talking about, *Valeria?*"

Valor gulps, wary of the Berserker's rage. I can't say I'm not either; Kian looks terrifying and it's not hard to see how he could fight off an entire army by himself.

Valor sighs, defeated. "I'm sorry. I swear, I thought you knew. I didn't realize until you told me you weren't blooded into the warrior Valkyrie before your clan was killed. If you were, you would know everything."

"What's everything?" I ask, teeth clenched.

"I'm a part of a sort of...intergalactic group of protectors. We're investigators."

"You have *got* to be joking."

"I'm not! You would have learned all about it—and joined, too—when you were inducted into the warrior Valkyrie."

"This is ridiculous!" Kian cuts in. "You can't actually believe it. It's nonsense!"

I look at him, and then look back at Valor. I see the truth in his eyes.

"I—" I break off. "I do."

Kian curses. He meets my eyes. "Why?"

I swallow, staring at him when I answer. "I trust Valor." And I do.

Valor's eyes widen and then go soft. He grabs my hand and squeezes. "Thanks, V."

Kian rolls his eyes. "Okay, so I guess Princess here has decided she believes you, so that's it. What does this galactic investigators club actually *do?*"

"The *Intergalactic Investigative Unit*," Valor starts, shooting Kian a look, "is a collaborative effort between the more *protective* species in the galaxy." He pauses. "Like the Gargoyle and Valkyrie. We work together to help combat problems that arise with other species.

I raise an eyebrow and wait for him to explain. My eyes are wide as I take in the abundance of new information. I can't believe my clan was involved in this. And a whole *galaxy* out there? Entire species I've never heard of? It's unreal.

"There's one species we've been investigating for a while, but we can't take them down. And we have no evidence because they're too good at covering their tracks. Their operation is extensive, widespread, and *clean.* They're everywhere." He sighs, pulling on his hair. "They have their fingers in every nasty pot you can imagine. They're sick and depraved. They need to be taken down. *Punished.*"

I get a churning feeling in my stomach. These...creatures can't be the ones that have my family. No way.

But I know I'm lying to myself.

"No," I say, starting to panic. "Tell me they don't have my sister."

Kian's eyebrows raise at my admission, but I ignore him.

"I'm sorry, V, but... I think they do."

AN HOUR LATER WE'RE SITTING in Valor's ship.

"So, you're *absolutely sure* this thing flies, right?" Kian asks again. For the fifth time.

"Yes, Berserker," Valor huffs. "I'm sure. My ship flies like a dream. It's top of the line."

"I find it *absolutely hilarious* that the big, bad Berserker is scared to fly," I taunt. Kian gives me a dark look. I raise my hands, resisting the urge to laugh at him. He bares his teeth at me when he sees my face, leans forward, and takes a huge bite in the air.

"Be careful, princess. I'm hungry, and I haven't tasted Valkyrie before. Maybe I'll just...sneak a bite." I roll my eyes. *What a psycho.*

"You don't scare me, *Kian.*"

He laughs. "Yeah, you're far too entertaining to kill."

"You're crazy," I mutter.

He opens his mouth to respond, but Valor cuts him off. "Shut up, Berserker. You're distracting me. You don't want me to crash, *do you?*"

Kian goes a little green at the suggestion and I laugh my ass off. Valor looks back at me and winks. I grin.

"Better strap in. Breaking through the atmosphere gives off a Hel of a lot of turbulence," Valor warns.

"Aye, Captain." I salute him and he smiles. Kian follows my lead, making sure he's buckled into his seat as tight as possible. He holds on to his straps with both hands, his knuckles turning red.

"Want me to hold your hand?" I smirk.

He narrows his eyes. I start to laugh again, but I startle when he freaking *grabs my hand* and squeezes. I open my eyes wide, and my mouth drops open in surprise. *Oh my goddess, a Berserker is holding my hand.*

"If you tell anyone about this, princess, I'll kill you."

I nod slowly. "Of course. I would expect nothing less."

The flight takes hours. In fact, I don't know how long we sit there. But Kian holds my hand the whole time. The second we stop moving and Valor docks the ship at our destination, he lets go, stands up, and pretends I never saw his weakness. *What an enigma.*

"This is The Outpost," Valor says. "It's a trading stop. It's...not a nice place. This is where *they* make some of their deals."

"What kind of deals?"

"Selling skin, mainly," he answers.

My lip curls with distaste and Kian curses.

"And these monsters have my family? My *sister*?"

"I'm afraid so."

"What do they want me for?" Kian wonders.

"Probably the gladiator fights," Valor guesses. "I'm sure a Berserker would be a great catch."

"Yeah, you're right. I'm pretty awesome."

I roll my eyes. "My goddess. You're incorrigible."

Kian winks. "You love it."

I ignore him. "How do we find them, Valor? Honor's been with them for six years. If they were sold off at The Outpost or another place like this, they could be scattered across the galaxy. We'll never find them!"

He sighs. "Yes, that's true. *If* they were sold at The Outpost, we'd never find them."

"If?" I ask hopefully.

"I believe they weren't taken here."

"Then why the Hel are we here?!" Kian yells. I'm inclined to agree with his question, but I'm sure Valor has a reason.

"Because we need to pay our way to where they are. You can't just show up at a place like this," the Gargoyle says through gritted teeth.

"What place? What *is it*?"

"It's called Aella. It's a Zoo. I think the missing Valkyrie were taken there. In fact, I'm almost positive. We'll need to go there if you want to get them back."

"This is going to be a lot harder than I expected, isn't it?" I ask, resigned.

"I'm afraid so, V." Valor sighs. "I'm afraid so."

WHY ARE YOU COMING WITH us anyway?" I ask Kian later.

It didn't take long for Valor to secure our passage to Aella, and now we were on our way there. Valor assured us that we'd need proper documentation to land, otherwise, we wouldn't have paid. I certainly didn't want to give *them* any of my money. Although, it isn't technically *my* money. Valor is the only one of us who has a real job anyway. Thankfully, he had no problems paying our way.

Kian didn't ask me to hold his hand this time, and I was grateful because I'm still not used to physical contact. Six years of being alone made me uncomfortable with touching. Although, I doubt Kian is familiar with it, either. A Berserker? Not likely.

"What do you mean?"

"Why'd you come with us? You've been running from them for five years. And now you're going right into the belly of the beast."

"I like to fight," he shrugs. "This seems like it'll be a good one."

"Bullshit."

He rolls his eyes. "Why does it matter?"

"I have my reasons," I say. He laughs, smiling as he remembers he answered the same way when I asked him why he wanted to know my name.

"Fine." He pauses. "Let's just say I have some regrets, princess. Maybe I feel like I should have stopped your Valkyrie from getting taken that night. Maybe I think I could have done more. Maybe it makes me sick that I let that happen. Maybe... I saw you that night. Making your vow. Maybe I wanted to stop that, too. Or say something to you when I saw how much pain you were in. But I didn't. Maybe I just want to help you, Valeria."

I swallow. I don't know what to say. I'm shocked. I feel vulnerable someone saw me that night. Exposed. So, I don't say anything. We sit in silence for a few minutes as Valor continues flying toward Aella.

I finally speak when he breaks eye contact. "Thank you for telling me, Kian."

He nods and then we pretend nothing happened.

I sigh in relief. There's been a lot of *emotions* since I met these two, and I don't know how to feel about it. It's so different from the past six years. I was stuck in the cold for so long—alone in the dark. Now, everything has changed again. Who will I be when I find Honor? What will she think of me? Who will I be *tomorrow*? I keep changing. Am I growing or descending further into darkness and chaos?

"We're here," Valor says.

"That was fast," Kian comments.

"I told you my ship is top of the line, Berserker," Valor says smugly.

"Whatever, Gargoyle."

"They'll check our documentation once I dock and then we can enter the Zoo. Based on my information, it's a series of glass enclosures with different exhibits. I haven't been inside yet, so I don't know all the details, but I'm told there's a lot of different species in here. Should be some of the rarest in the galaxy: the strongest, the most beautiful, the most exotic, the most interesting."

"Can I see my sister?"

Valor shakes his head. "I don't think so, V. They'll know right away you have a connection. You're identical. Even if your hair is white and your wings are hidden. They'll know you're Valkyrie."

I sigh. "Hel, you're right. I know. I just...want to see her. It's been so long."

"I know, V. But you'll see her soon. We'll get her back." He squeezes my hand, and it hurts a little less. "Just remember, we're on recon only."

"Okay, fine. I'll be good."

"I doubt *you* have the ability to *be good*," Kian says on a laugh.

I roll my eyes. He's probably right. But I won't be admitting to anything. Kian smirks like he knows what I'm thinking.

"Let's go," Valor calls out as he walks to the front of the ship.

Kian and I follow. I steel my shoulders, preparing myself to enter Hel. My sister is here. I feel it.

The door opens and we shuffle out. My eyes open wide when I see the large, ornate entrance. Guards meet us at the bottom of the dock and quickly check over our documents. They review the rules, repeating what Valor told us earlier and my eyes sharpen when I hear them. It's disgusting how apathetic they are. One of the guards' eyes linger on me and I resist the urge to squirm, sidling closer to Valor and Kian instead.

"You're free to go in," the guard says. "Have fun."

Kian grins darkly, and the guard swallows, sensing the danger in the Berserker's eyes. He laughs and we walk through the gates, entering the Zoo where the Valkyrie and other unwilling captives are held.

"Where do you think they are?" I ask.

"No idea, V," Valor answers. "Let's look around. This place is huge."

We stop at the first enclosure, and I look inside. It's a perfect garden sanctuary. A paradise. But I know it's just a facade. Because there's nothing about this place that doesn't run thick with toxic fumes. It's poison. And I intend to make them all bleed.

I see screens set up all over the walls surrounding a large glass picture window that show different views into the sanctuary. On one screen is a bathing pool and resting inside of it is a creature I've never seen before: a female with a long fish-like tail.

"Mermaid," Valor says before I can ask.

"Wow," I breathe.

We move on to the next enclosure, and the next, and the next. We don't find the Valkyrie.

We finally arrive at the last two enclosures in the hallway, and I see a girl. She's beautiful. Definitely exotic, but also less so than some of the other creatures we've seen. No wings, scales, or fur to be seen. She has white-blonde hair and perfectly grey eyes. She's wearing a white dress, but

I see markings all over her arms that remind me of my sigil, making me think she's not used to dressing like that. She looks like a warrior.

I walk a little closer and I notice she's crying. For some reason, I want to help. I feel a strange connection to her. One that I can't explain. I turn towards Valor, intending to ask for something—I don't know what—when a bestial roar interrupts me. It's *loud*. I've never heard anything like it. Valor's mouth drops open in astonishment and Kian's eyes light up with excitement.

"Holy Hel, what is that?" Kian yells as a beast breaks out of the trees. The giant, black beast breathes fire, burning down the glass walls between his enclosure and the girls', then he snatches her up in his claws and flies away. Up, up, up into the sky. And they've *escaped*.

"We need to find them right now," Valor says.

"What?"

"We need to go," he insists. "We need to make contact before they leave Aella."

"But—but my sister!"

"I'm telling you, V. They'll be able to help. I promise."

I sigh. "Okay, fine. Let's go."

Kian whoops and we head out, walking as fast as we can without raising suspicion. It takes thirty minutes to make it back to the entrance of the Zoo. Ten more minutes to make it to our ship. Ten more to take off.

And then we're zooming through the skies, searching for a sign of the beast and the girl.

An hour later, I find them. "There!" I point to two figures on a mountain and Valor directs the ship and lands.

Valor lowers the ramp and opens the door. I peek through the doorway, seeing a large male pushing the smaller female behind his back. I hear her talk to him, trying to push her way to stand beside him, and I laugh quietly.

The male must have enhanced hearing, though, because he turns at the sound and gives me an assessing look. "What do you want? We're not going back to that place."

I walk down the ramp, Valor and Kian trailing behind me. "Trust me, I'm not with them. I don't want to take you back. Although, I can't say I don't *want* you to *want* to go back."

"What?" the male asks, confused.

"What do you mean? Why would you want us to go back?" the girl finally speaks up.

I raise an eyebrow. "Isn't it obvious? They have something I want."

She crosses her arms. "Like what?"

"My sister." I pause. "And the other four remaining members of my clan."

"Clan?" she asks. "What are you?"

"That's not a very polite question, little girl," Kian says.

I slap his arm. "Don't call her that, Berserker." He grins.

I roll my eyes. "I'm a Valkyrie."

She purses her lips. "You don't look much like a Valkyrie to me."

"And what would you know of the Valkyrie? What are *you*?"

"Human."

"Human? You're from Earth?" Valor sputters.

"Yeah, so?" the human girl stands up straighter. I laugh. I like her.

"Listen, we saw you escape, and we thought you might be able to help, that's all."

The girl shares a look with the boy she's with. I realize he has the same color eyes as the beast. He must be a shifter. One I've never seen before. Valor must recognize his kind, though, to have been so keen on teaming up.

"Well, maybe we have a vendetta of our own," she says.

"Really?"

"Yes," she responds. "I think we have quite a few things in common, Valkyrie."

I grin and point to myself. "I'm Valeria." I point to my companions. "Valor and Kian. My *associates*."

Kian laughs. "Come on, princess. We're friends." I roll my eyes.

The girl laughs. "I'm Addison Rose and this is X."

"Nice to meet you." I pause. "So, human, huh?"

She smirks. "Yes. Basically useless, but I get by." She laughs. "Valkyrie, huh?"

I smile and come to a decision, making eye contact with Kian, and winking before answering with my truth.

"**Ég** hefna mín."

My wings burst from my back in a shower of blood and sacrifice. Knives sharp enough to pierce the skin of my enemies. Blades I can throw with my will. Strength. Power. *Mine.*

I notice Valor looking at me reverently like he did the first time, but Kian's gaze is all hunger. I ignore them both and focus on Addison Rose, curious what she thinks.

"What does it mean?"

"I am vengeance."

In her childhood, long before current airline security measures, Heidi Moone narrowly missed an opportunity for a mid-flight tour of a cockpit. More importantly, she would have received a pair of pilot's wings. Fate twisted another direction, but she's never forgotten the beautiful silver wings which could have been hers.

Little wonder then she writes a story about a lady balloonist who earns her wings during the American Civil War.

WINGS, PRAYERS, AND BLACK POWDER

Heidi Moone

THE WEATHER OUTSIDE THE MEETING hall was ungodly, with wind lashing the timbers of the building as though evil deeds were taking place within that a vengeful Deity might be opposed to.

Probably, Ernesta Blanchard thought, this was only too true.

She knew she was young for this type of business, and she was not respectable. However, she believed in herself, in her skills, and in her equipment, and when word had gone through the community that there would be, of all things, a commission involved in the United States military, well, family honor was at stake as well.

"Ernesta, I find myself unsurprised to see you here."

The voice, which had come from behind her, did not cause Ernesta's heart to jump, but rather to sink like ballast. She turned her head back to take in the lovely, even enchanting, Miss Eliza Gardner.

With hair as dark as midnight, eyes as blue as the sky, and even two dimples, Miss Gardner was Ernesta's superior in both age and reputation. Her family had enjoyed great renown in France, and all over the Continent, and while she had changed her name with her arrival in America, the trace of a French accent only served to make Eliza more charming than ever.

Ernesta had seen many of the male balloonists swoon over her in the past, and their stupidity deepened once they realized her skills with parachuting.

For her own part, Eliza never seemed to encourage any of these unfortunates, and was entirely talented and professional. Rumor had it she was being pursued romantically by some sort of robber baron's third son, but there was decidedly not a ring on her finger at the moment.

"Miss Gardner, I could say the same, I suppose," Ernesta pressed her lips together. "You don't seem the sort of person who would be enticed to come here."

"Before all else, I am a patriot," Eliza replied, a little stiffly.

"How could one question such a thing?"

Ernesta turned to see Claudine Sutter standing there, looking scornful as she approached her best friend in the world.

If Eliza was elegance and grace, her constant companion, Claudine, was steel and sarcasm. They were friends, as their mothers had been friends, and their grandmothers. They were inseparable, to the point that Ernesta doubted they even knew which of them had decided to make the journey to America.

Unlike Eliza, Claudine's French accent was more pronounced.

"Eliza, has this person been a nuisance?"

"We must remember our manners, my dear, as I believe we may all be facing an enduring companionship before the night is through," Eliza noted in a practical tone.

That was likely to be true, considering this had been a summons to the capital, Washington.

Ernesta, lacking any real desire to agitate the soldier she knew Claudine to be, went and knocked smartly on the door. Rap-rap-rap. Pause. Rap-rap. Pause. Rap-rap.

An unfriendly man opened the door, and he was clearly looking above Ernesta's head. Finally, he thought to lower his gaze, and his unfriendliness thickened. He said nothing at all to them, apparently having given up manners to join the military.

From her coat sleeve, Ernesta produced a plain white envelope with a wine-colored seal on it.

"I come at the invitation of General McDowell," she said.

"We all do," Eliza's voice echoed. Doubtless, they had similar invitations. "I would like to know the meaning of such disregard."

"We can't be too careful," a dry, masculine voice sounded from behind the guard. "These ladies are, indeed, awaited within."

The soldier's lip curved into the shadow of a sneer as he stepped aside for Ernesta, Eliza, and Claudine.

Within, a gentleman awaited, by the cut of his clothes, far too good for a common soldier. Ernesta had an eye for cloth, and she knew good tailoring when she saw it.

"Captain Lazlo Kiss, a pleasure to meet you once again," Eliza said, proffering her hand as a lady might. The captain inclined his head over it, and then smoothly stepped back.

The little dance of the well-to-do, Ernesta thought with no heat, nor any particular warmth.

"Captain Kiss?" She tried not to look surprised by the name.

"My father was Hungarian, it's a common enough name there," he said with a grin and a bigger smile in his dark eyes. "You must be Ernesta Blanchard. Your pedigree is impressive."

"I am not particularly impressed by it, but if you choose to be, I cannot stop you," she said, and with a swish of her skirts, she followed in the wake of Eliza and not-at-all-charmed Claudine, who had offered neither hand nor name to the Captain.

There were enough men waiting for them in the room they ended up in that Ernesta was confident they would not be taken at all seriously, but she had been in many such rooms in her life, and it wasn't how you walked in, it was how you walked out that mattered.

At the head of the room was a woman of color. Her hair was stylish, but her attire was more akin to a man's than a woman's, which was perhaps unseemly? Her head was tilted to one side, and she smiled as the women appeared.

"Finally," she said, her accent quite different from the French Ernesta had grown up speaking, and yet harkening back to it at the same time, like a dream, "we can begin this matter properly."

"How exciting," a lightly-accented German voice said, belonging to a grey-eyed girl who looked rather sickly. "And you are all three of you bal-loonists?"

"I am Ernesta Blanchard, and I am a professional balloonist," Ernesta said at once, squaring her shoulders.

"I am Eliza Gardner, I am both a professional balloonist and a professional parachuter," Eliza followed on her heels. "And I present Captain Claudine Sutter, retired of the French army, who is more than proficient with ballooning, but doesn't consider it a vocation."

"Captain?" One of the men up front snorted.

Ernesta, apart from this not being her particular battle to fight, already knew how proverbially outgunned the scoffing young man was.

"I saw service in Morocco and Algiers," Claudine said, her tone nonchalant. "If you have any questions regarding my proficiency with sword or pistol, we can discuss your concerns at dawn."

"Do it," one of the men next to him egged him on, but the man who'd spoken up looked at Claudine for a long moment, and then held his tongue.

Smarter than a first impression would indicate, then. Ernesta had seen Claudine duel, once. To say she was vicious would be understating the matter.

"If we're quite finished," a man stepped into the center of this, "I am General McDowell, and I'm the reason you ladies are here this evening." He frowned for a moment. "There are supposed to be more of you."

"You didn't send me a list of people to bring with, and I'm hardly interested in being a nursemaid," Eliza said, looking at her glove. "General, if anyone is tardy, perhaps we should presume absence equals disinterest."

"Mrs. Wilkes has written, sir, she is unable to attend this evening," Kiss offered.

Ernesta wasn't surprised Mrs. Margaret Wilkes—and what other female Wilkes could they possibly mean—had chosen not to come. She was eight months pregnant at the moment, though Ernesta wouldn't mention it to any of the men hereabouts.

"Clementine Barrow is, sadly, unable to be in attendance as well, as she has suffered an accident a few days before," Eliza said. "I would hardly think you would convene a meeting of professional lady ballooners without her."

"Is she on the mend at all?" Ernesta asked.

"One can only hope the surgeons don't have at her, in which case she can potentially recover nicely," Claudine murmured.

One of the men in the room, presumably a surgeon, or fond of them in some respect, harumphed notably at that statement.

"I wanted at least four, and preferably a half a dozen candidates," McDowell noted.

"Explain what's needed of us, and we can make recommendations if we're not sufficient for the task," Ernesta suggested. McDowell looked at her a long moment, and then nodded, seeming to make up his mind on the matter.

"We have attempted this with your male colleagues, and have been disappointed," he began. He stopped, and when none of the women interrupted him, continued on. "Precisely speaking, the leadership in this conflict we find ourselves in believe that aerial reconnaissance, perhaps even more active activities, may help with the effort."

It was the war effort, then. Ernesta looked across at Eliza, who was solemn-faced.

"You have tried the gentlemen colleagues we're aware of, no doubt," Ernesta heard herself say. "And what's become of them?"

"Failure. Downed balloons. Accidents. We have had disappointment after disappointment, despite early promise."

"And now you wish to employ women in the same job? I believe in my own competence, but I required a reason," Eliza said. "If it is to cast aspersions on my gender for failure, sir, you may look elsewhere."

"Everyone is aware of the situation in Europe," McDowell said abruptly, looking at Ernesta.

Ah, that.

"The European theater is very different in a number of ways," Ernesta began.

"Your grandmother has been a stalwart part of the French air command since Napoleon's days," McDowell said. "Your mother's actions were legendary in Spain."

"And you have invited me in the hope of some brilliance having transferred," Ernesta swept at her skirts, Eliza's frown now on her face. "Sir, I am the black sheep of my family, and while I do enjoy a great deal of familiarity with ballooning, I am not natively martial."

"I suppose you wish my skills with both ballooning and parachuting for the same reasons," Eliza sniffed. "It is no easy thing, what you desire. Not every man, nor woman, is suited for such work, General. I think your ambitions outstrip your reason."

"And if the others were here?" Kiss asked.

Ernesta's mind turned over and over.

If she had been in different company, she might've confessed to feeling somewhat faint at the audacious lie she had just told.

Her eyes slid across to boards covered with cloth. Ah, to look underneath, at the secret plans plotted by those in power. The military men who would always rule the world with cunning and violence.

Her mother, who disapproved of Ernesta's hunger to take to the field of battle, had told her that the shedding of blood was nothing to yearn for.

"When you see someone's life leave their eyes, Ernie, you'll understand," she'd said as she had efficiently cut her youngest daughter out of consideration for the French Air Command.

"What would our test be, all that being said? And what would our compensation be?" She asked McDowell in a quiet voice. "I was not born in America, but I come from one freedom-loving country to another, and I see no particular objection to the pursuit of peace and freedom for all the peoples of this land."

"The freedom of all peoples is not the purpose of this war," the man she thought might be a doctor or surgeon spoke up, cutting across the conversations that had begun. "The continuation of our great, united nation is the very heart of this cause."

Personally, Ernesta thought that was a pretty bold statement to make when there was a black woman in the room watching them all, patient, waiting for a moment to act.

"Imagine, peace to all men," another man in the back chuckled, but Ernesta grit her teeth and turned back to the General.

"We would offer no more, nor less, than we had to your gentlemen counterparts," McDowell explained. "Command of a formal air division of the military, with a full commission, pay, and authority."

"My demands would be pay equal to that offered to the gentlemen, if I do acquiesce," Ernesta said. "And if you are faithless, General, I will be aware of it. I know the men you had been working with."

"Many of them are dead," McDowell was blunt.

"And their wives," Ernesta continued.

"Are you entertaining this?" Eliza asked her.

"I confess, I feel this is no favor being asked of us, Miss Gardner. However, I cannot deny a certain interest."

"So much for being the black sheep," Claudine murmured, but she had an approving look about her.

"If you write to my mother and grandmother, they'll be happy to entertain you with tales of my unsuitability for many things," Ernesta was hardly troubled as she looked at the General.

"What is the test you would put us to? If it is hazardous, or risks our precious materials, we would need remuneration even if we are ultimately not selected for this service."

"I remain against this, McDowell," a young man to Captain Kiss' right spoke for the first time. "Women are of chancy temperament at the best of times. It's inconceivable that they would succeed where civilized men failed so completely."

"On the Continent, all this work is left in the hands of women," McDowell said. "They are lighter, and the balloons bears their weight more easily, according to the literature. Their flighty dispositions on the ground become more rational when they are higher in the atmosphere, where the thin air improves their minds as it robs men of their wits entirely."

With some effort, Ernesta suppressed the (doubtless) hysterical laugher that was inclined to bubble up inside of her.

Really, when she had some leisure time, she would have to peruse 'the literature' written about her kind.

"How can it hurt for them to make the attempt," Kiss noted, his voice smooth, calming. "We would not put them into harm's way, Dunlop. They simply would need to put on a demonstration, and these ladies all have experience with that."

"Are you also a balloonist?" Eliza asked the black woman who had since approached her, a measuring tape in hand. "If it please you, for we haven't been introduced."

"I am Miss Royale Sinclair, and it pleases me greatly, Miss Ernesta Blanchard. I found it interesting to know you'd Anglicized your last name." She began to measure Ernesta in a variety of ways, quick, experienced.

Perhaps she was a seamstress. The ballooning crowd did have to deal with more types of cloth than was worth mentioning.

"It seemed the thing to do in an English-speaking country," Ernesta nodded. "And you are not a balloonist at all."

"I could not be enticed to go into such a contraption," Miss Sinclair said blithely. "I have a formidable fear of heights, but a love of the science involved. I am a scientific consultant, you see."

Ernesta wasn't sure she did see, but she didn't know politely how to go about stating her puzzlement. She, herself, had spent so much of her own childhood in the air, and while she respected great heights, a life spent separated from them would be unbearable.

"Do you have your equipment at hand?" She asked Eliza, who shook her head.

"Everything I have is in Boston, currently," she said. "Not here in Washington."

Ernesta, in fact, had never launched out of the capital city either. She worked out of New York.

"Ladies, we have some things for your consideration," Miss Sinclair smiled. "General, I'll be taking them with me, I believe."

"You have my complete confidence," the General said, and they found themselves swept from the room filled with men in a different manner from the one Ernesta had anticipated.

OUR WORK HAS BEEN CARRIED out in the greatest secrecy," Miss Sinclair noted as she hurried them out of the carriage they'd taken from the meeting hall. Claudine Sutter seemed to have little patience and less curiosity, but Eliza was quiet and set on accompanying this new woman to their destination, and Ernesta was decidedly intrigued.

"Did you work with any of the men the General had originally approached?" She asked instead of the myriad of other questions swirling in her aching head. Another one of her headaches was imminent, and she would need to find a dark room to take her medicine in, sooner rather than later.

"Those men were very invested in their own inventions and self-worth," Miss Sinclair mused. "The few who were intrigued in our work seemed intent on 'borrowing' it for their own purposes. Sadly, the General is fully aware of what our division has been working on, and so when those men presented our ideas as their own, they were swiftly locked away."

"Locked away?" Eliza looked alarmed.

But Claudine smirked.

"War time secrets purloined would suggest they could be enticed to spy for the enemy," she said. "I'd have shot them at dawn, personally. War is softer, nowadays."

"Oh my," Miss Sinclair said, her eyes wide as she took in Captain Sutter where she leaned against the wall rather nonchalantly.

Then she knocked at the door they'd stopped at, thrice, then thrice more after a pause. A lock could be heard turning, and a freckled, youthful face appeared.

"Royale, however did it go?"

"Pauline, I have returned with new balloonist recruits, if you would only use your eyes," Royale said with something of a grin. "Everyone, I would be delighted to introduce you to Pauline Phillips, she is the ward of my fellow inventor Daniella, and something of a tinkerer in her own right."

"How rude of you, I am very brilliant," Miss Phillips declared, her eyes dancing with both merriment and a dash of indignation. "Hello, ladies, a pleasure, I am sure."

"This is Ernesta Blanchard, she is from the first family of ballooning in France, she has changed her last name," Miss Sinclair continued. "Eliza Gardner, you will know her from the parachuting, of course. Her boon companion, Captain Claudine Sutter, lately of the French armed forces."

"Oh my, distinguished," Pauline did look the most impressed with Captain Sutter. "Have you murdered anyone, Captain?"

"As many people as I rightfully could," Claudine replied without batting an eye. "Gruesomely as well."

"And that's enough of that," a voice from within beckoned them, and they went through the door to see what lay within the proverbial lair.

Inside, was nothing short of a warehouse, and within that warehouse were inventions uniquely devoted to the science of air travel.

Ernesta sucked in air, and then more air. She frowned.

"That is a fixed frame vehicle," she observed of the balloon hovering about twenty feet away from her.

It wouldn't hold more than a person, and of course she had seen such things before. The problem being, Ernesta had never operated one before, nor had she a particular fondness for such devices.

"Let me look at it more closely," she heard Eliza say, her tone entirely different. Of course, for all that Eliza adored ballooning—she was no amateur—she loved parachuting more. Eliza's demonstrations, as she called them, invariably involved more and more elaborate means of descending from balloons to the ground in relative safety.

"You aren't a fan of our work," a voice came from behind her, and Ernesta turned to see a honey-eyed woman standing there.

She was intelligent, Ernesta felt at once, and not even because she wore the accoutrements of someone who could build a fixed frame flying machine, and sporting a tool belt around her waist, and goggles haphazardly pushed onto her forehead.

She seemed to have wheels turning even as she stood there, taking Ernesta in, and the former Frenchwoman frowned a little at the intrusion, which made the stranger smile.

That smile transformed her face from the everyday to something memorable.

"I am Daniella, and it is an absolute pleasure," she said, her honey eyes containing little flecks that almost scintillated as she stepped in to offer her hand. "I know you are Ernesta Blanchard now, is that correct?"

"It is," Ernesta nodded. "I won't be tedious and ask how you knew."

"Such a delight, you've no idea," Daniella's smile brightened a notch. "Please speak freely. At some point tedious, small-minded men will appear and make life dreary, and until then, we should let our minds be free."

"I prefer non-rigid balloons," Ernesta said at once. "I adore them. I have experience with rigid airships. They are not my favorite."

"Fascinating. I believe that rigid-frame will allow us to proceed with directional movement, but I'm delighted to find someone with the expertise to contradict me," Daniella said.

"Miss…" Ernesta was at a loss, she did not have a last name to fall back on. Daniella laughed.

"There is no Miss for me, I am simply Daniella," she explained.

"How can you not have a family name?" Ernesta blinked.

"I did away with it. Highly recommended," Daniella nodded. "Come with me, the other balloons are this way."

They trotted down, their boots making clattering noises as they crossed thin sheets of metal.

"I am impressed with your workspace," Ernesta noted.

"It's been a struggle to gain acceptance and resources. The war is a terrible circumstance to take advantage of, but there is opportunity in misfortune," Daniella said. Ernesta noted that Eliza and Claudine had followed in their purposeful wake.

There was a half-wall made of wood, and beyond that, in a state of deflation, were balloons that Ernesta could immediately recognize and appreciate. She approached the nearest one, frowning at the dull colors.

"Not exactly the sort of contraption I work with normally," Ernesta mused, crouching to run her hands over the balloon surface.

The material felt like silk coated in rubber, which was reasonable, if still not optimal. Was it coated on both sides? What was the mechanism for heating the air, or did they prefer gas? Such matters were of constant interest to balloonists.

"We have night balloons and a variety of daylight balloons, all in suitable colors. I do admit we didn't fuss over it much, and those things were chosen by the gentlemen who had previously been engaged to work on this project," Daniella explained.

"Were you frustrated?" Ernesta asked. "I'm surprised to find women in charge here."

"Respectable engineers aren't engaged in aerial foolishness, or so I was told," Daniella said, her tone unflaggingly cheerful. "It's an opening an enterprising young miss might crawl through, if she notices it's there at all."

"And your purpose in fighting in this war?"

That had been Eliza.

"My purpose is to challenge the systems of slavery in the South," Daniella revealed. "You'll find Royale's answer to be the same, though she can speak for herself, and will."

"You aren't concerned about the Union?" Claudine asked, and Daniella chuckled, quite a chilling sound, really.

"Men put things together and then pick them apart once it doesn't suit them," she said with a shrug. "If women had made the country, I might be a little more emotional, but no. I dislike things like slavery and injustice, and since America is so fussed about such things in the first place, they can stand to have these things offered to all the people who reside here."

"She's a suffragette," Royale explained as she walked up with Pauline, who had a tray filled with tea and cookies. "As am I, but one step comes before the other."

"Having a vote when you have no liberty seems ridiculous," Claudine nodded. "I am not inclined to support slavery, of course. Our country despises it, despite our love for America."

"You don't consider yourself American," Daniella seemed amused, and Claudine shrugged.

"Enough of such things," Eliza said briskly. Ernesta happened to know Miss Gardner was not particularly enamored of things like the universal right to vote despite one's gender, but to see such daylight between her and Claudine was unusual. "What is this test we're to be put to?"

"Ladies, I can answer that," Captain Kiss said, stepping out from behind the wall. "Miss Sinclair let me in, before you can scold me again, Daniella."

"How familiar of you," Eliza sniffed.

"Daniella has only the one name," I said, and Eliza's eyes widened in some degree of horror. "Daniella, please make the acquaintance of Miss Eliza Gardner and her companion, Captain Claudine Sutter."

"Two Captains in my company," Daniella mused. "I rather do fancy that, how does it make you feel, Captain Kiss?"

"I declare myself to be unperturbed," was the man's reply, and Ernesta wasn't troubled by that, she found. "Now, the test is straightforward. We wish you to take a balloon—we have almost a dozen of 'em—and go on a simple scouting mission."

"You want us to spy from the air, and then what, return signals to the ground? What will we spy upon?" Ernesta frowned. This wasn't what she'd been expecting at all.

"You will spy upon the enemy," Kiss said. "We have anticipation of a great battle to come, sadly not long in the future, and not far from where we are, and we would have you spy on the enemy and determine their movements. Yes, it comes with danger. This is no simple test. We don't have the men to spare to design any fake test for you."

"Well, you could employ the walking wounded in the hospitals here in Washington," Daniella mused, and Kiss frowned at her while she smiled at him.

"McDowell has made the arrangements," he said. "There will be a special train that will take us to the wagons we've arranged for. The battleground, we believe, will come to us in Maryland."

"So close," Eliza murmured, Kiss had not lied about the proximity of war. Ernesta felt, suddenly, vulnerable in what she had considered to be a perfectly safe city.

"We leave in twelve hours, or we don't leave at all," Kiss said with a shrug. "Pick your balloons, anything you need, I will see that you get it, if it exists."

"He meant that for me," Pauline explained after Kiss had turned and strode off, with Daniella walking alongside him, their heads bent together in earnest conversation. "Do you know what balloons you would like?"

"The rigid-frames may not be ready for this," Eliza told Ernesta, her lips pressed together. "What are these made of?"

"It looks like silk with rubber," Ernesta said. "I would have transported my own balloons if I'd realized what we'd have to work with here."

"Is there a problem?" Royale asked. "These were constructed of material we've had shipped from India."

"Oh, I've no doubt the silk is sound, but I didn't see the stitching before it was coated," Ernesta explained. "And for my part, I have concerns about how the rubber may burn, while the lacquer I've invented for coating cloth is far superior."

"Does every balloonist have their own methodology?" Pauline seemed quite intrigued.

"I have never met anyone in our business who didn't," Eliza smiled, a tight smile. "My own concoction, which I hold to be far superior to Ernesta's, is also not a base rubber over silk."

"We don't have a lot of time," Claudine noted, taking off her coat. "Let's get everything sorted, then, shall we?"

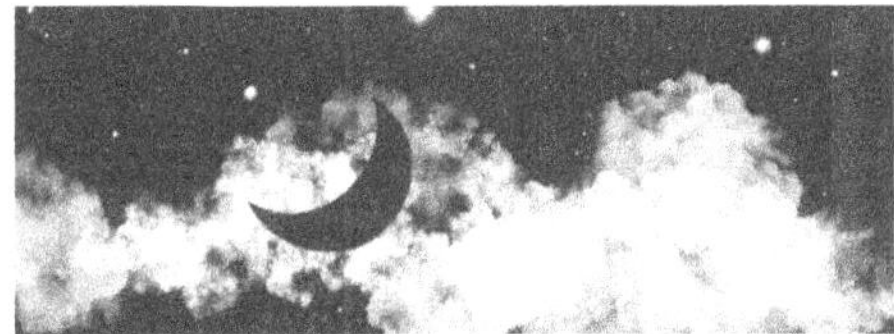

TWELVE HOURS LATER, THEY WERE being bundled onto a train car.

In that time, they had tested as many of the balloons as could be inflated, tested, and then the prime candidates had been deflated once more. A process that might take hours had been accomplished far more quickly due to the technology provided by Royale, Daniella, and Pauline.

Yes, Ernesta thought, they were all now on a first-name basis. She ruffled her clean skirt—her belongings had been fetched from the boarding house she'd selected for her stay in Washington D.C.—and frowned as Pauline finished plaiting her hair.

"It'll be out of the way," the younger girl said ruefully. "Your hair is magnificent, Miss Blanchard."

"My thanks, Pauline," Ernesta said. "But you may call me Ernesta, if you would like."

Pauline blushed and then grinned and ran off to tinker with one of the heating devices that might keep her alive, or cause her ruination and death.

"You seem composed," Eliza noted. She had her own hair braided back into a tight bun, and Claudine was examining a firearm she'd been handed, quietly, by Daniella. It seemed rather small for a proper gun, and made of brass, to boot.

"It's a day in the air," Ernesta said, her voice not even tight. "Where I belong, if you ask most people who are acquaintances. How are you feeling?"

"If this is indeed a reconnaissance mission, I have few qualms," Eliza said. "The men shoot terribly under most conditions, I've heard, and we shall be high in the sky and not any immediate threat to them."

They had chosen two different types of balloons. Eliza was to operate a semi-rigid balloon that would be filled with hydrogen gas. Dangerous, but so very useful, she would also have to wait for the balloon to finish filling.

Ernesta had chosen a traditional balloon, and Daniella had taken two hours to instruct her on the use of their new device, a gas-powered engine that would blow heat out a tube on the end. It would be suspended by chains, as the device could get hot, she'd been warned.

Nothing about this was promising, but it seemed far superior to the other flame-producing options she had. There would be no open flame near the balloon itself.

And the engine was attached to another device that might provide directional movement, although this was less likely. Examining the winds as she looked out the window to the dawn's early light, Ernesta thought they might, at least, be going in the right direction.

"'If this is a reconnaissance mission, I have my doubts we will be particularly impressive to many people," Ernesta admitted. "And while this intrigues me...is this something I would want to do with my life?"

"Are you so against the direction your family has taken their own lives in?" Claudine asked.

"It's more complicated than it appears from the outside," Ernesta frowned, but at that moment, Daniella appeared and stood before them.

"I need to borrow Miss Blanchard, Ernesta, for a moment," she said. "We will arrive within the hour."

"Excellent, time for a nap," Claudine decided. That woman could sleep anywhere.

They went into the next car, which held her balloon, partially inflated already. When they arrived, the roof would open up to release it.

"I've made the preparations you've asked for," Daniella said, looking serious now. "Ernesta, I've had to inform Captain Kiss of your intentions."

"It's more a precaution than an intention," Ernesta said. "I am not convinced that simple reporting of troop movements would be satisfactory for a demonstration."

"

IT'S ALL THE GENERAL ASKED of the gentlemen," Daniella shrugged. "And even then, so much woe and calumny ensued that they're still straightening things out."

"Were people really thrown in prison?"

"In fact, yes. The concern was that they were spies, if not merely loose-tongued fools," Daniella winced, looking anything but pleased. "I confess that I miss none of them."

And then Ernesta looked to see a second balloon in the long car, next to the one she'd selected.

"A backup?" She asked, curious, and Daniella turned to her, smile restored.

"Among my many inclinations is a fascination with ballooning as well," she admitted. "It was an informal pastime in my family, and we are not as illustrious as your own, I assure you."

"So, you intend to be the third balloon today," Ernesta was surprised.

"I do. I feel this will have a greater chance of success, and continued funding, if there are three balloons in the air today. The original intent was to have four or more, but not everyone responded to the invitations," Daniella explained.

"Yes, I know of a couple of other people," Ernesta frowned. "They might join us later. Or this could be a fool's errand. Thousands of years of war, and balloons have been involved in them for less than a century."

"If there will be advancements in civilization, I fear they will come through warfare," Daniella said.

And from there, they discussed strategy and tips until the train arrived at its destination.

Ernesta was impressed with how confidently Royale directed sullen, sulky young soldiers to preparing the area set aside for them—which meant it had been overtaken by several soldiers who'd taken their field for a napping area.

"Rouse yourselves, or we shall crush you," Royale advised the men, who were inclined to use foul language directed at her.

Fortunately, Miss Sinclair also had a walking stick with which she began to clout the worst of the offenders, and Claudine sauntered over to make her presence known, which caused the troops to slink off.

"I appreciate that their necks will be on the line shortly, but that doesn't mean they have earned the right for coarse insolence," Royale grimaced a little as she made her way back to where Eliza was testing the platform she would be riding on.

She had, at least, brought three parachutes with her, all encased in a light back worn on the back. She had encouraged Ernesta to take one, and finally, the encouragement won out over the fear of never having tried such a thing before.

"You will activate it by this cloth," Eliza showed her. "Pull violently to force it from the bag. Your life will depend on it functioning properly."

"Lovely," Ernesta said.

"I have designed it and practiced it on more than one occasion," Eliza said, gesturing at her own pack.

Claudine also wore one, but that left nothing for Daniella, who professed to not mind in the least.

"I intend to not need such a contraption," she said.

Well, no one intended to parachute, besides insane people who liked to descend from a balloon to the ground below, and people whose lives were in mortal danger.

"I thought it would be bulkier," she admitted.

"The silk is so fine, and coated in a formula I've spent years perfecting," Eliza said, looking proud.

She and Claudine were both dressed scandalously in trousers, while Danielle wore riding skirts, which seemed somewhat practical. Ernesta, her balloon finally ready, and the winds just so, looked at the clouds in the sky, stepped into the basket—a proper basket, at least, and examined the devices hanging from it.

"What are you going up with?" Eliza asked.

"Well, perhaps it's nothing. I just wanted a little surprise, should any of us be targeted," Ernesta explained.

"Unlikely to happen," Captain Kiss said as he strode up, an aide scurrying alongside him. "This is purely for you to monitor troop movements and communicate them down to us."

He then proceeded to hand them a half-dozen flags and start walking them through a variety of signals they were to flash to the aide down below, who would be watching and waiting to send runners with instructions.

"The time to walk us through flag signaling was probably last night," Eliza yawned.

Claudine looked unworried, and Daniella had paid no attention at all, so presumably she had this strange system down pat. Ernesta frowned. She had retained portions of what Kiss had hurriedly explained, but she couldn't take an additional person into her balloon with her.

And so, she grabbed the flags, stepped into the balloon, and dropped her ballast. Her balloon lurched into the air with little effort at all, the people disappearing in a very satisfying way.

Ernesta inhaled deeply as the balloon went up, and up. The wind took her, and she employed the engine to try and direct the forward motion of her balloon, feeling the whup-whup of the fans as they fought to take her somewhat against the wind.

But a balloon would not behave like a boat, she thought, and in short order she found herself drifting, but at least in the right direction, looking at the color differences between Union and Confederate battalions.

"This is ridiculous," she thought, sorting through her brain to remember what flag meant what when held a certain way.

And in that moment, merrily moving past her like she was standing on a sidewalk, went Eliza's egg-shaped balloon, with Claudine crouching in the middle of the platform like an angry cat, while Eliza leaned from the ropes as though in her element.

"You've done well with it," Ernesta said, and though she didn't call, her voice may have carried, because Eliza turned and grinned at her in a fashion that would've even put Daniella to shame.

Speaking of which, she saw Daniella's balloon now, moving straight to the west, and either the lack of weight favored her, or the engine she had was superior, because she was decidedly moving against the direction of the wind. Impressive!

There was a flash, and Daniella was waving flags like a champion. Ernesta puzzled them out, but by the time she had one position pegged, Daniella had flashed several more. Down behind them, in the field, she could see the tiny figures of the soldiers like ants, scurrying about.

Then she saw Claudine get, gingerly, to her knees, and also begin to wave her flags, based on what Eliza seemed to be telling her.

Enough of that. Two balloons feeding information would be more than enough, Ernesta decided, and she set her course directly toward the closest Confederate line, to the south.

She could see, even if she didn't know the flags to wave, that there were troops in grey marching toward a Union line, and she felt that this was something worth signaling. She grabbed up two flags and, hopefully, flashed a signal that said South-Confederate-Troops-Advance, and then nursed the engine that was very unbearably hot into moving her balloon more quickly through the air.

Ernesta was quite high up as she floated across the creek, and saw some of the Union troops, already engaged with the enemy, look up in astonishment at her balloon. Then she heard an unwelcome sound—gunfire.

Were those cads shooting at her? Looking down, she wasn't sure what side the bullets were coming from, but no damage seemed to have been down. Her lip curling a little, she leaned out over the other side of the basket, to see that indeed, a column of men were marching quickly toward the fray.

"I am born for this," she said to no one in particular, or perhaps she was just letting God know, because now Ernesta took up the first of the ordinance hanging over the side—as far away from the heat as possible—and recalled Daniella's instructions.

"When you have need of it, cut the fuse to estimate, light, and drop."

Daniella had marked the fuses, and Ernesta looked down, estimating her distance from the men below. Some of them seemed to be excited, and then she realized why—her balloon was grey, like a cloudy day, and they wouldn't think this a Union balloon, would they?

The soldiers would've loved her performing balloons, Ernesta thought. She liked brighter colors when she wasn't about to disrupt enemy plans.

She cut the fuse with her pocket knife, and then lit it using the engine. Wasting no time, Ernesta dropped it over the side, not even breaking a sweat, as she had handled black powder in her fireworks displays for many a year.

Down, down, not on the men—Ernesta wasn't sure she had the taste of blood for that, quite—but in front of them, designed to scatter and intimidate them.

Then the explosion came. It quite rocked the basket she was in, and Ernesta tumbled a little bit, even against the backdrop of cannon fire and tumult from below.

"What did you give me, Daniella?" She had bit her tongue, and Ernesta scrambled to look down to see a crater in the ground below, and shocked, horrified little people all gesturing at her now.

Yes, she absolutely had their attention now.

There were no Union troops coming to challenge the new arrivals, and so Ernesta grabbed the next of the ordinance, cut the fuse, and threw it, lit, over the side when she felt she was well-positioned.

By now, the Confederate troops had taken up a defensive position, and were no longer marching headlong into the fracas north of them. However, some of them had begun trying to shoot at her balloon. Ernesta took it higher by pushing the engine, but the fuel would hardly last her the whole day if she kept on at this rate.

She only had six of the bombs left, and in short order, to keep the soldiers pinned down, she was down to two.

Waving a flag seemed rather useless at this point, the field was so far behind her, and in the distance she saw Daniella's balloon weaving back and forth over the thick of the fighting, and further north Eliza was maneuvering her airship to some purpose or other, but it was much too far for Ernesta to discern what might be happening, or if help was needed.

By now, the Union forces had overcome the Confederates at their position, and none of them seemed to be shooting at her, so small victories.

At that moment, the entire balloon shuddered, and then lurched violently. Ernesta grabbed the basket—false promise of security though it was—and looked up to see flames blossoming along the edge of the balloon.

What had gone wrong? Was it the engine? She looked at the thing, but it was operating as it always had, nothing seemed amiss with it. More likely, the material had a weak point that the heat had finally wore through. She'd seen it more than once in her career.

Ernesta would have time to land safely, even with the fire, only she was above the Confederate troops, and this didn't seem a steady plan in the least.

Pulling up the remaining two bombs, she cut one quickly, lit it, and dropped it below. The other she left uncut, lashing it to the engine, and lit it where it stood.

Now, her life was in Eliza's hands. Ernesta leapt up to the rim of the basket and jumped out without giving much hesitation. At least the engine would not fall into unfriendly hands. She hoped Daniella and the others would understand!

The explosion from below buoyed her up, and she was weightless in air for a long moment, as though she might be suspended in the water, and then Ernesta pulled violently on the parachute mechanism, feeling the air ripping at her as she hadn't since she'd been a child, up with her mother in a balloon that had failed, leaving them hurtling toward the ground.

In that case, their balloon had been caught on the branches of a large tree, and they had not died, to the astonishment of many. When the tree had finally given away, the water beneath it had been their final cushion of life.

Now, she had nothing but silk and prayers, and perhaps not even the silk.

She pulled, and nothing happened for a long moment. But then the bag fell apart, the seams revealing a thin ravel of pale pink silk that formed into a wide parachute, with a hole in the middle, to prevent the dizzying spinning that could come from inferior designs.

So elegant. Ernesta sucked in breath as her headlong plummet turned into something less horrifying—though she then had to tuck her own skirts down somewhat, and lamented the lack of men's trousers!

With a little bit of effort, she found that she could at least steer the parachute a little, and then came to a rough landing—she rolled—on a hill some little way away from the Confederate troops she'd tried to bedevil. Looking up, she could see the remnants of the balloon falling toward where they had been, and it was rather a heartbreaking thing.

She hadn't known that balloon well, but she had enjoyed flying it. And certainly, her return to earth had been anything but dignified.

Fighting her way out from underneath the silk, she bundled it up quickly, the better to leave nothing behind, and then began to wobble off in the vague direction of the Union troops, before thinking the better of her plan, as she doubted they would know what to make of her, and one of them might just opt to shoot her rather than ask pertinent questions.

"You are something of a fool," Ernesta told herself, coming within sight of the creek. And now, she could swim across, or she could follow until she found a bridge or a boat to help her get back to the eastern side.

THREE HOURS LATER, AS THE sun crept toward the apex of the sky, some Union soldiers came across her, and Ernesta was surprised all over again.

"We have located her!" One of them declared, and another came up and saluted to her, looking very excited.

"You're a marvel, no doubt about it," he said. "You were the one, right? In the balloon?"

"I'm one of the ones," Ernesta said, and the men proceeded to escort her to what turned out to be a staging area, complete with a tent, and someone in charge. She spoke with the Colonel, who said he'd been asked to look for her, and then to alert Captain Kiss to her whereabouts.

"You are the hero of the moment, Miss Gardner," he said. "Word has come that you prevented a good portion of the army's march from Harper's Ferry. We're quite pleased, to say the least."

"Oh, yes, they were moving very quickly," she said, unsure of what Harper's Ferry might be, or even quite where she was at this point. "Have the other balloons stayed in the air?"

"They have returned to the eastern banks," one of the men said to her, rather respectfully.

"Is it true that your grandmother fought for Napoleon?" One of the other men asked her after the Colonel had turned away to arrange transportation for her.

"Well, yes," she nodded. "And my mother and aunt are involved with the French government now, of course."

"We're mighty pleased you wanted to come to America," another said.

"Liberty is liberty everywhere," she murmured, but Ernesta was a little overwhelmed by the enthusiasm, and pleased when she was given a mounted escort over a bridge, and in short order found herself in the presence of a bemused Captain Kiss.

"The men are going to be talking about you instead of their well-earned wounds," he speculated. "The balloon going down in flames was seen for miles around, you know."

Ernesta groaned as she was helped into the carriage that had arrived for her.

"I will find a way to compensate Daniella and Royale," she offered.

"Did the engine go down intact? It's important to know," he said once he was seated beside her. Fortunately, another of Kiss' aides was seated there, so there would be no perceived impropriety.

"I set the last of my ordinance on the engine and lashed it there. The last explosion was the engine," she explained, and he nodded, looking satisfied.

"The General has been quite pleased by the demonstration. It's been determined that the Confederate advance toward Washington has been halted, and it looks as though there will be a retreat back from Union territory, which has been quite helpful."

"You possess a talent for understatement," Ernesta sighed, looking out the window. "Did the others actually accomplish the assigned task?"

At least, if two of the three balloons had done well with information collection, this might not be a complete failure.

"Yes, they remained in the air. Neither of them were involved with the enemy. But Miss Blanchard, I must say, you successfully held up the march of reinforcements from the south in a way none of us quite imagined possible. Everything I'd heard about your family, and more, has been validated."

Her finger drummed on the window of the carriage.

Her mother would hear of this. Of Ernesta's decision to, well, throw explosives at a hapless enemy below.

Of course, they were hardened troops who had themselves seen battle, who had cannons, guns, and a determination to invade. This was, after all, a war, not a heated verbal dispute of some kind.

"It needed to be done," she said softly.

"It was brilliant," the aide ventured, and Ernesta turned and smiled tightly at him, worried at his enthusiastic face.

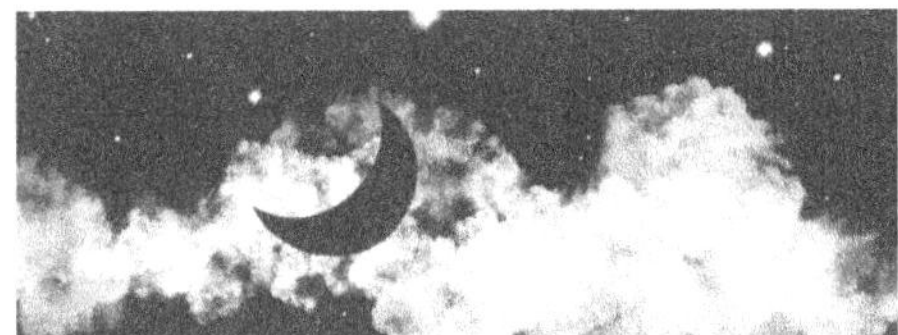

BY SUNSET, THEY WERE ONCE again in front of General McDowell.

"The signaling was quite essential, and we had several troop maneuvers happen entirely due to the intelligence relayed from the balloons," he began. "For that alone, I would continue to invest money into this unusual venture."

Off to one side, Daniella, who had singed some of her hair off, and nursed a burn on her left hand, was hugged by an enthusiastic Royale.

"The fact remains, the troop movement to the south being stalled thanks to the stalwart efforts of Miss Blanchard, word has reached the President himself, and he was most impressed. We're having an etching done even now, and sent to all the papers."

"Oh my," Ernesta said, not sure what else to say. Yes, there would be no hiding this from her family in France.

"There can be no doubt that we have had a telling victory. The fighting is still fierce in pockets at this hour, but the wind is out of their sails, and the Confederates are sulking back home, having been given a drubbing they'll remember for some time. And at the hands of a lady." McDowell was anything but displeased. "You've outdone the men, and confirmed my faith in you ladies was not misplaced.

"It is true what they say, General, in the air, a female mind is superior," one of the other officers spoke up.

Ernesta, at a harsh look from Eliza, bit her tongue fiercely.

"And so, it's with great pleasure that I intend to offer you command of the air," General McDowell explained, taking a box from the officer who had just spoken. "You will be Air Commander, a rank equal to General, of all Union forces. The President has called for you to be known as the Aeronautics Force, a new division of the military, from this hour forth, comprised of a female force of ballooners, and support persons."

"Oh my," Ernesta said, with much more feeling. The box opened, and there, resting on a velvet blue cloth, lay a beautiful set of outstretched silver wings, belonging to an eagle resting on a star with a balloon in the background.

As she held it up for the other women to see, the moon burst out from the clouds that had threatened all day, and set the wings aglow.

Eliza stepped over and nimbly pinned this dramatic thing to her collar.

"We'll work out the uniforms after," she breathed into Ernesta's ear.

Of course they would. While this lasted, because this would only be a temporary advancement. But what had been done couldn't be easily undone.

"The troops are quite excited, we will give you funding for a good dozen balloonists, we will have need of you on multiple fronts," the General was explaining. "Congratulations, Commander."

"Thank-you, General," she said. "We need to, ah, return to the warehouse—will we have a place to headquarter and a budget?"

"The President has already authorized it. You'll have a communication from the Treasury tomorrow," McDowell explained.

She already was sorting through her head, wondering if she could entice one of her cousins over from France. If she did this—and she seemed to be doing it—there would be much more work than her firework displays in Boston would ever offer.

"Brilliant," Daniella said, and Eliza looked excited.

"I rather wasn't expecting a…commission?" Ernesta frowned, running her fingers over the tips of the eagle's wings. They were sharp, and would draw blood if she didn't mind them.

"The moment I heard the first explosion, I was hopeful," Royale said. "The troops with us, here on the ground, could talk about nothing else. They feel this will change war forever."

If that would be the case, Ernesta decided at once she would have to remain in charge in some respect. It would likely all go wrong regardless, but she could try and make sure someone with a conscience stayed at the helm of this Aeronautics Force, as long as it might exist.

If Elizabeth Knollston could have wings, she'd choose silent wings. Perhaps it is not so odd then that the Huntress in her story doesn't hear the danger of an avian predator until it is too late. Moonlight and wings in the heart of an ancient forest, and nothing is ever, can ever be the same again

THE BONE TREE

Elizabeth Knollston

THE LACK OF MOISTURE TURNED the forest floor into a labyrinth of impossible moves for the Huntress and her companion. Leaves, curled and devoid of life, lay scattered across the parched dirt. Low-hanging tree limbs snapped and popped as they passed. Bushes, typically laden with fragrant flowers and berries ripe for harvest, reached out with spindly skeletal arms to snag their clothing.

Chardra stopped and squatted. She shook her hand in disgust at the sweat wiped from her brow. "There is nothing here."

Her companion stopped by her side. "We should have traveled south with the other villages. Our people can adapt."

"And leave our traditions? How is it I argue from where you should be standing?"

"The currents would move with us," Eli snapped, more in response to the sting of sweat in his eye than the well-worn argument between them. "The Upright have shown us."

Chardra held up her hand, fingers clenched into a fist, silencing Eli. Her head and upper body tilted forward; eyes focused on a dying cluster of bushes a few yards in front of them. The last of its leaves were not enough to camouflage the animal moving behind it.

With practiced control, her hand moved to her side and pulled an arrow from its quiver. She shifted her weight to her left foot, her right leg sliding out to compensate. Despite Eli's initiation as a Keeper of Ritual, the training received as a child had not gone to waste. He held still, slowed his breathing, and channeled his focus to Chardra.

Squirrel chatter broke the silence, and the deer bolted. Desperation forced Chardra to loose her arrow, even though the Huntress knew there would be no kill.

She sprang to her feet and kicked at a pile of leaves. "Curse this blight!"

Eli waited for her temper to cool.

"Am I to return empty-handed to our village? The Knife has sent all her hunters, and we return with barely a scrap worth feeding to the hounds." She whirled around, deep brown eyes filled with self-loathing. "Why have we been so mistreated? Why has the forest forsaken us? Does not the Upright have a response to those questions?"

Eli reached out for her hands and pulled her to him. He leaned in and touched his forehead to hers. "The currents still flow and are everlasting with lessons tucked into these experiences we have yet to perceive and understand."

Chardra shook off his embrace. "That is not enough." She stepped back, a frown etched onto her lips. She was the Huntress, the one the Knife turned to for counsel. She was the one all other hunters aspired to be. It was Chardra who knew where to scout for the fattest prey, who understood the rotations of the seasons and the ebb and flow of what the forest could provide. It was Chardra, parents went to when a child wandered too far into the forest and didn't return. And it was Chardra who the Upright considered a suitable replacement for the Knife when the time would come.

"Perhaps it must be." Eli bent over and picked up a leaf. One-half brown, easily destroyed when touched, while a spark of life still clung to the other half. "Life has both a beginning and an end. Neither is complete without the other. The world turns in seasons. Fresh new life gives way to mature abundance to the silence of the Deep Darkness. The Knife teaches all her hunters the rhythm of movement inherent in the game you seek. Perhaps it is time for our people to experience a new cycle. Death to what we have been, and rebirth to what we will become."

"I will not abandon our home. Nor will I trade it for the villages of the South."

"Do you condemn our child to a life of hunger and want?"

The question was sharp. His words found purchase and wounded her.

Chardra's hand moved to her belly, touching the spark of life within. "Do not tell me of the bounty promised in the South. You know it is the land of the Forgotten. I have seen the brittle bones of those who live and trade amongst them. I will not see our child forced to live such an existence."

Eli dropped the leaf and looked off into the distance.

Chardra could no longer face him and turned away. Their argument was well worn and often traded among their village. Too many leaned towards the lure of the South, and too few honored the connection in their bones to the forest. Either path forced their child to face a bleak future, one of hunger, or a loss of connection to who and what they were. She closed her eyes and dipped into her memory.

The Knife had risen and greeted her in the gray of the morning before she and Eli set off on the hunt. "It is a kindness the Upright have sent your partner with you on this task, and not another of the Keepers of Ritual. You are the best our village has produced in many cycles of life. If you do not return with a source of food, I will have no choice but to listen to the song of the South."

Feeling the growing chasm between herself and Eli, Chardra was not sure if it was kindness Eli now traveled with her, or an underhanded attempt by the Upright to manipulate her emotions.

"The dangers are less in the South."

Chardra tensed, this was a new approach. "Danger is all around us. This is why each village has a Knife and her hunters."

"There are dangers inherent in the forest which will not be found in the South."

She scowled and twisted to look at him. "If you speak of the tales the Keepers have spun into lessons for our children, do not use them to support your position."

Eli did not reply.

"We will move on." She was grateful for his silent obedience.

The forest was an extension of her body, and she took comfort from its familiar touch, even as it lay parched and dying. Every hunter spent a cycle of life, living on their own within its embrace. How else were they to learn its secrets, remember its hidden paths and discover the bounty it had to offer? Moving through tangled branches and exposed roots brought Chardra to life. There had never been another path for her. From the moment her eyes had opened and her senses had shaped the world around her, the forest had called to her.

The sun dipped towards the horizon, and Chardra came to a stop along a small trickle of water. The stream held barely enough to dip a hand within and find a sip to relieve their parched throats. Eli found a seat amongst a cluster of mid-sized rocks and pulled out pouches of food. Each had been sent with enough to see them through the turning of the moon.

He handed Chardra her portion and partook of his own. "I do not recognize this area."

Each village that called the forested land their home maintained a boundary for its hunters. These men and women knew to keep to their own, and only move into another village's boundary with permission from the Upright. The blight had forced many of those villages to lay in ruin and abandonment. On this hunt, the Upright permitted free movement within the depths of the forest.

Chardra swallowed and shrugged. "We are beyond the boundaries. Two days past the Turning Stone." She ate a handful of nuts. "To the west is what is left of the Ramc Village, the east is the Atwa, or what is left of its mighty waters."

Eli had been her chosen partner for well over five years. An unusual choice for a hunter, but the spark danced between them and each read the other well. A gift she now regretted. She noted the unease beneath his words, the furrowed brow. Had he been a part of the decision to come with her? What had been the motive of sending a Keeper along on this hunt?

Their opposing views were well known in the village. Yet, they had each been able to respect the other through the tightening emotions of their people. Eli was not without standing among the Keepers of Ritual. Could his journey with her be a way to secure his position? To show the Keepers he had the power of persuasion if they returned and the Huntress sanctioned the idea of moving South?

"How much further do you choose to take us? Should we not move towards the Atwa? Surely game would move along its banks, looking for any water that might be left."

"This is not the first time you have tried to steer my course, Eli." She recalled the numerous questions and observations he had spoken since they had left the village.

"Nor will it be the last." The man stood and stretched. "Will we camp here?"

If there was an unseen current running through his actions, Chardra could not yet tell.

With narrowed eyes, she answered. "No, we continue."

Annoyance flashed in his eyes, and his lips turned down before he masked his emotions from her. Despite the unease settling between them, she did not press. They had withstood many disagreements, and she knew they would withstand many more. He would tell her when he was ready.

The moon's bright light provided the path she chose. Despite the unfamiliarity of her surroundings, Chardra moved with purpose. A purpose soon rewarded.

She stopped and crouched down. Dung and the faint outline of a hoof. The forest life around them held still in the glow of the moon's light. Where decay filled the day, the moonlight reversed death's severity. A few yards ahead of her were bent branches of a young sapling. As she moved forward, her hands brushed the dirt, tracing another faint hoof print.

Further ahead, she found more dung, more prints. The dung was dry, but not yet covered in the beetles and flies which thrived on it. The herd had to be only a day or so ahead of her.

"We will continue on tonight. With luck, we will come across fresh tracks by mid-day. If the currents are with us, we may have game by evening."

When only silence answered her, Chardra turned and discovered Eli had not moved forward with her. She gave a low hiss, not wanting to waste the time. But she could not leave him. He would be lost now they were beyond their village's boundaries.

Retracing her steps, she found him staring at a bird's nest which had tumbled to the ground. A glance told her the nest held no eggs to be harvested, and annoyance bubbled up inside of her.

"We must move on. There is evidence of a herd further ahead."

"No."

The reply was swift and brutal.

Eli turned. "We must turn west, towards the Atwa. Whatever game may be ahead of us is not worth our efforts. The game will have moved to the mighty waters of the Atwa. That is where we must go."

Chardra took a step back. His words were firm. Spoken as a Keeper of Ritual. This was not her Eli watching her. Taking her measure. But she was the Huntress. An extension of the Knife, of the surrounding forest. They were standing within her domain, not his.

"The Knife has already sent our hunters towards the Atwa. They returned with little. I will not repeat such a mistake."

"We are too far into the forest."

"Do you not trust me?" The question had been preying on her thoughts, and it came forth before she could stop it.

The mask of the Keeper remained for a moment, and then it dropped as Eli blushed and looked wounded.

Chardra closed the distance between them and touched her forehead to his. "I do not know what the current has in store for us. I only know what I can see with my eyes, smell with my nose and touch with my hands. The forest will provide. I must follow what it tells me."

Eli brushed his lips against hers and laid his hand on her belly. "I know. Yet I fear for what it might reveal."

He pulled back and held up a feather. It was long and wide and black as the longest night of the Deep Darkness. Its edges were well worn, as if the bird it had belonged to suffered from some type of disease.

If that was his concern, she would ease his fears. "A bird and beast do not always carry the same diseases. If I were to fell this bird, I would burn its carcass. All hunters are taught the signs of sickness. You should know this."

"Can you identify the bird which carried this feather?"

The question was an insult. An inquiry a Hunter would make to a child, to ensure they understood the beasts and birds which shared their home.

Yet this was Eli. Her lover which asked; a man who would not insult her. She searched his eyes, and found no hint of jest within them.

"It is of the night predators, most likely a variety of the black taloned birds."

Eli glanced at the feather with pursed lips but did not continue the conversation. She watched as the feather slipped from his fingers and floated to the ground.

"Come. By tomorrow I am hopeful we will have found what we need."

Chardra turned and together they moved deeper into the forest.

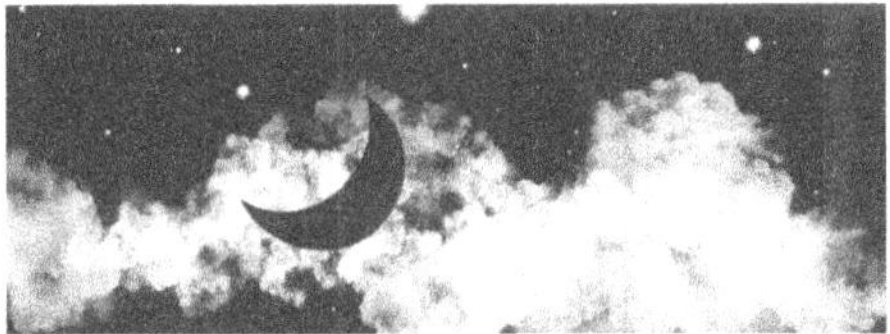

BY THE TIME THE SUN crested the horizon, Chardra was losing her patience with Eli. Too many times throughout the night, she had retraced her steps, only to find him examining more discarded feathers, or asking if she had heard strange animal cries.

Many in the village aspired to be a hunter but found themselves quelled by the tremors. Either a natural disposition to fear what the depths of the forest concealed, or a superstition born of listening to the stories told at night.

Chardra had patience with those afraid of finding a predator lurking, waiting to catch its prey off guard. Wildcats and night stalkers would gladly devour human flesh. There was no shame in admitting this fear. What good would it do to provide the Knife with hunters too timid and afraid to supply their people with the meat needed?

Eli was not such a person. The ability of the hunt was within him, but his mind had been attuned to the ways of the Keepers, just as Chardra's had been to the forest. She needed him, for his physical strength and mental clarity. When they came across the herd, she would need his help to strip the hides, prepare the meat, and build a sled to bring the meat back to the village.

"Eli," Chardra hissed.

Her agitation grew as he turned and walked off from her. This was no place to be lost. Chardra was following what the forest revealed to her, and the tales told by the Knife. Stories shared to prepare her hunters in case they found themselves too far past the boundaries. Chardra had no other option but to follow.

Eli moved as if there were no forest working to impede his steps until, at last, he stopped. Chardra gripped his shoulder and forced him to turn, to face her. The look which befell her sent shock waves through her body. Her hand fell, as if scorched by fire, and her body instinctively backed away.

It was a look of sorrow she had never witnessed upon his sturdy countenance. Tears coursed down his cheeks, and a feral look of fear guarded his eyes.

"We will find what we seek." Her voice faltered. "I know the forest will provide. Our people," she touched her belly, "our child will be taken care of."

Eli did not reply with words, but with a gesture. He turned and tore at a clump of vines, holding on for dear life to an upheaval of stone. Chardra carried basic knowledge of the art of healing. What she knew was designed for the physical wounds she might encounter on the hunt. There were no physical wounds here. This was a wound of the internal, and Eli needed the council of the Upright.

Eli clawed and pulled at the vines until specks of blood smeared the stone underneath. Chardra's heart grew fearful. She could not leave Eli here, nor could she care for him and still fulfill the needs of the village. It was a rare occasion in her life when she felt lost and unsure; traits which were deadly to a Huntress.

Vines tangled around his legs, Eli stopped. "We have come too far. Too deep. Too close to the night of Ethwam. We must turn back." His fingers left bloody prints on the stone's engraved images, long since dulled by the rains.

A tree, its trunk and limbs bare, had been carved into the middle of the stone, and was surrounded by birds, chosen to be depicted as entities as large as the tree itself.

Eli crumbled to the ground, and indecision rushed from Chardra's body as she closed the gap between them and caught him. She pulled him into her lap and wrapped her arms around him, gently rocking back and forth. She hummed a simple melody all mothers whispered to their children at night, until at last, she sensed the tension drain from his body.

"Forgive me. My mind and body struggle with the sacred duties of the Keepers."

Chardra stilled and listened. Keepers guarded their knowledge, sharing only what they needed to perform their duties for the village. It was their honor to guide the village in the remembrance of the sacred days, to be a voice for the Upright, and to counsel those on the blessings of the currents which surrounded them.

In her concerns, she had not considered what meaning it might hold for Eli, for the Upright to have him join her on this hunt. Chardra had only seen it as a way to quell her disagreement with moving to the South.

"I can feel it in my bones we are nearly there. We will harvest the game and then return. This journey is near the end."

An odd look of shame and fear passed across Eli's face before he pulled out of her embrace and rose to his feet. "Do you know what you see before you?"

Chardra stood and brushed the dirt from her trousers. "It is a stone."

"Look beyond the surface of your eyes. Look deeper into the currents."

Seeing such sorrow written upon his face scared her. The impatience and fury she had felt only moments ago vanished. Eli was a Keeper, and she could feel his need to have her listen.

The stone was taller than Eli and wider than the two of them put together. "Is it another of the Turning Stones?"

"It is, but not a Turning Stone of the Knife, of all those who join in on her hunt. It is a Turning Stone of the Upright. This is the place where we must turn back. To step beyond this is to venture into the Heart of the

Forest. To the source of the currents which guide us, surround us. You must hear this and understand this. To venture beyond this point is to journey into the paths of the Upright."

His words carried weight. Chardra listened, tried to understand as he repeated his warning, his fingers tapping at the carven images. This was a sacred place, a sacred moment. She knew the stories, she understood the duties of the Keepers. Their stories were meant to teach, to guide those of their village. But she was the Huntress. The forest was composed of earth she could feel beneath her feet, wind across her skin, the scent of life. These were things she could touch and taste. His stories were not.

"If this journey was after the night of Ethwam, you would not need to so carefully consider this. Yet this night will bring the full moon, a reshaping of our world into another."

There was a deeper current Eli was encouraging her to see, yet Chardra was swept back to the needs of her people, of her child. She respected the knowledge of the Keepers, but this was not the time for stories. Her focus was on the direct consequences of the blight.

"Then we shall complete the hunt before the rise of the moon. The sun has only now begun its ascent. We can secure enough to bring back to this spot and prepare it here for our return to the village."

If there were more words Eli wanted to speak, they did not come. Only, "It is the choice of the Huntress."

"Do you trust me?" the question forced itself to be spoken one more time.

Eli stepped forward and grabbed her hands, bringing them to his lips, to his forehead, and then to rest against the steady beat of his heart. "I trust you. And I will walk this journey with you."

The show of affection, of devotion, caused Chardra to shed tears. "We will find the food we need for our people."

She pulled back and turned, moving off in the direction they had come. His words weighed heavily in her mind, yet with each step forward, she felt the forest welcoming, embracing her just as it had as a child. This was her duty to her people. She heard the warning Eli had issued, the sorrow beneath his words. His words were those of a Keeper, and she did not take them lightly, but in her heart, she knew this was the path she must walk.

The trees became thicker, older and the blight which had driven them so deep within its heart had not touched the trees here. Branches hung heavy with life and more than a few carried sweet and juicy fruit. Even the light of the sun found it difficult to penetrate such thick foliage and Chardra felt her heart lift as she moved from shadow to shadow, the Huntress closing in on her prey.

Rich, moist dirt revealed fresh tracks, and Chardra stopped and held up her hand. "Stay here."

Eli crouched down within the crook of an old tree and Chardra began the hunt. She could sense the group of deer just beyond the next clump of bushes, and she opened her senses to the forest. Life flourished all around her, from the insects beneath her feet to the birds and squirrels above her. Noiselessly, she crept forward and gained a line of sight on her prey. While not yet fattened for the Deep Darkness, there was enough meat to secure the approval of the Knife for another hunt.

Chardra could see it with her mind's eye.

She and Eli would return victorious. The Knife would send her with more hunters to the Heart of the Forest, and they would secure enough to see them through the lean cold months. She had not been oblivious to the fruit, nuts, and berries she had passed. While not a normal part of a hunters' duty, they would harvest what they could of those as well.

Her village would not move to the South. The blight would pass, and life would return to how it was.

Chardra notched her arrow, others ready to fly mere seconds after the first and took aim. Her arm pulled back, her breathing slowed, and her fingers released their hold on the arrow when a scream flooded the forest.

Its pitch was high and piercing, forcing Chardra to drop her weapons and cover her ears. The horrendous scream came again and again. The deer scattered; her prey lost.

Despair and anger surged within her and then fear buried itself in her bones.

"Chardra!"

She ran, crashing through the forest back to where she had left Eli. If only she had checked to ensure he carried a knife or a weapon to defend himself. Wildcats were not known to stalk their prey in the heat of the day, and night stalkers were more common towards the western part of their village's boundary. Yet the blight had forced many to hunt in unusual patterns.

Chardra burst through a tangled knot of branches, only to stumble and fall at beholding the scene before her.

A bird, larger than any she had seen before, had Eli in its grip. Its wings moved with precision, keeping its body aloft as its talons sunk into Eli's shoulders. Blood poured from the wounds and stained his tunic. With each push and pull of the bird's wings, its talons ripped deeper into his flesh, until Chardra could see they had gone clear through his shoulder.

This was no ordinary creature of the forest. This was a nightmare come to life.

A Devourer.

Her hands closed around the leather-bound hilts of the knives tucked into her belt. Footing regained, she picked her target and let the blade fly. It struck the bird, its point digging deep into its back. A cry of outrage pulsed out of the nightmare.

Even as the scream stripped the forest of its peace, Chardra charged the impossible predator. Muscles tensed, she lept. Eyes fixed on the base of the bird's skull. A wing swept open and back, knocking her to the ground. Her body rolled, and she slid into a crouch, ready to spill its blood.

The bird touched its beak to Eli's forehead and a gust of wind ripped through the trees. Debris pierced her exposed skin, and it forced Chardra to raise an arm to protect her face. When the storm subsided, she looked. Ready to reassess her attack.

Her blood ran cold at what she saw.

Delicate strands of blue light pulsed between Eli and the bird, cocooning them in a tightening web of complex lines. Each pulse drained the color from Eli's skin until it was ashen and increased the intensity of color among the bird's iridescent feathers.

Fear rooted Chardra in place as the Devourer took her beloved's life force. The tales of such creatures told to all village children sprang to life. Stories describing the woes of children who disobeyed their elders, and received a visit from the Devourer. A creature who lived to strip others of their life force. Whose malevolence spread like a disease, trapping and tainting the surrounding currents.

In the cold of the Deep Darkness, hunters embellished their adventures with glimpses of such a creature. Or encounters with other such beings who held importance only in the teachings of the Keepers.

This was no story.

This was of flesh and blood.

The Devourer pulled back, its beak lifted to the sky as it let out another scream, a cry of victory. It tore its talons from Eli's body, and with one sweep of its massive wings, took flight.

There was no time to mourn. If this nightmare truly existed, so did the chance of reclaiming Eli's life. Chardra took off. Instinct and years of experience allowed her to race through the tangle of roots, limbs, and vegetation while tracking the bird above.

While her body raced through the forest, her mind shredded any concerns for her village and landed on one thought. Vengeance. She would destroy the one who had destroyed her beloved, her companion, the father of her child. She would shed its blood until the earth turned bitter.

The Devourer maintained its northern journey, and Chardra did not stop as the sun moved across the sky and dipped down to take its rest once more. Senses fully opened, there was no barrier between her and the currents she moved through. Life scurried and scuttled through the darkening landscape, most resting with the disappearance of the sun, while sharp eyes marked her progress as moonlight flooded the earth.

As the moon hung bloated and heavy with promise, the Devourer descended. Chardra slowed her pace and examined her surroundings, noting terrain and potential weapons. The forest had thinned, trees becoming narrow and spindly. Leaves hung in odd clumps, the moonlight highlighted their jagged edges. Strange and ethereal birdsong filled the cool, damp air. As she crept forward, her legs brushed against tall stalks on which hung jewel-toned flowers. Their perfume floated along the cool breeze until Chardra could not only smell them but taste them as well.

The Huntress had found the Heart of the Forest. She stilled and took in the view. The trees stopped a few feet ahead of her, their branches bending back towards the darkness of their brothers and sisters. Beyond stretched a meadow of dew-kissed grasses, sparkling in the moonlight. Yet it was what lay at the center of the meadow which drew Chardra's eye.

Extending up from an earthen mound was the Bone Tree.

If she had not witnessed the Devourer, she would not have believed.

The Bone Tree of white

The Bone Tree of light

The Bone Tree's bite

To speak the words was to invoke the wrath of the Upright. It was taboo, only the Keepers could discuss such topics. Yet, it was whispered of late at night, when the fires had burned out and families returned to their homes. The Bone Tree. The center of the Heart of the Forest. Where all currents sprang from and returned.

It was the ritual of death. A ritual all villagers were aware of, yet none partook in but the Keepers. When a villager died, their body was laid to rest within the embrace of a tree's roots. Flesh would rot, a feast for the creatures of death. Roots would entangle and pierce the bones, capturing the life force within and sending it through the underground network of tree roots, to their forbearer, the Bone Tree.

As Chardra's mind grasped the gravity of what the forest revealed to her, doubt gnawed on the edges of her thirst for vengeance.

Eli's words whispered in her ear. "If this journey was after the night of Ethwam, you would not need to so carefully consider this. Yet this night will bring the full moon, a reshaping of our world into another."

The rituals and celebrations of her people were pleasant, yet not a topic her mind often settled on. The Keepers saw to what needed to be done to appease the currents, to maintain the balance of the village with that of the forest. Those of the Knife were trained to hunt. Not to sit around the fires and discuss the meanings and importance behind the beliefs.

A pang of sorrow and fury intertwined as this would have been the time she needed Eli's counsel. An unfamiliar emotion, small and insidious, flared to life. Guilt. If she had listened to Eli and turned back at the Turning Stone, he would still be alive. If she had listened, her child would still have a father. Her remorse fed the guilt until it spilled over into her tears.

In her grief, she missed how the forest grew silent as a great shadow blotted out the light of the moon. Muscles tensed as she sought to steady her thoughts, to regain control over her mind. The Devourer landed next to the Bone Tree.

From her vantage point, she had not realized the size of the Bone Tree until the giant bird composed of nightmares stood beside it. Its trunk was thicker than the breast of the bird, and its limbs stretched far and wide, as if reaching for the stars above.

A flock of roosting birds took flight off to the right of Chardra's position. She twisted to see them rise above the canopy of the forest and head south. Moments later, another group called out and winged their way through the night sky. All together, Chardra witnessed five groups of birds disturbed from their nests. Each group was progressively closer to her position.

Something else was moving through the forest.

She backed deeper into the shadows, still maintaining line of sight with the Devourer. And waited. It did not take long. A dark oily shadow poured out from the forest's edge close to her position. Its slick exterior absorbed the moon's light as it spread through the meadow and moved towards the Bone Tree.

Sickness filled her belly as the gelatinous mass slithered up the mound and embraced the base of the tree. The Devourer hopped back and forth on its massive feet and its beak clacked in eager anticipation. The inky shadow stretched up the Bone Tree until it wrapped the entire trunk in its horror. The Devourer trilled, and then the shadow pulled back and sunk into the ground.

Chardra turned and vomited.

It was to be a night of horrors.

Yet, if her mind had not been so consumed by vengeance and grief, she might have recalled the Devourer's companion. Nor would she have left Eli's body unguarded.

She should have listened. She should have heeded Eli's warnings.

Standing against the pale, smooth bark of the Bone Tree, was a skeleton.

The bones of Eli.

The Devourer deprived its prey of the sacred days of Passing, when a life force was transferred through the roots of the forest, returning to the source of all currents. The Ravager was drawn to such a carcass marred by the unnatural death, and together they created a mockery of the sacred Bone Tree.

Bile burned her throat as she forced herself to turn back to the grisly scene. The limbs of the Bone Tree shook and trembled as if caught in the fury of a storm, yet all Chardra felt was the gentle breeze with the scent of night.

Eli's skeleton stood tall against the Bone Tree and Chardra knew there was still a chance of reclaiming his life force. Seeing the Devourer and the Ravager in the flesh sparked the memories of tales whispered when she was a child, huddled around the fire at dark, listening with wide eyes as her elder brothers talked of the time before the Devourer.

In the Age of Silven, it was believed the Bone Tree flourished. Its buds ripening into jewel-encrusted flowers. The perfume of which spread throughout the forest and brought peace amongst all who lived within its shadow.

When the nightmare tore through the land, it grew jealous of the Bone Tree and devoured its jeweled flowers. Its appetite not satisfied, it pecked and clawed at the Bone Tree, breaking its limbs until nothing but a mere shadow of itself remained. The nightmare was not without intelligence and pierced its great skull with a piece of the Bone Tree, so it too might taste the sweet nectar of a life force.

There was no time to consider, measure, or plan. There was only time to act. To trust in the training she had received from the Knife since a child.

Chardra was the Huntress.

Her body exploded from the protective shelter of the dark woods. Her feet dug into the soil, finding purchase amongst the grasses of the meadow. The cry of the Huntress tore itself from her body, filling the night air. A challenge to all who would dare threaten those she loved.

The Devourer turned, its yellow eyes gleamed with delight as its fresh prey run towards it. Its massive beak opened, and it met her challenge with one of its own. Wings wider than two men opened and pushed it into the air.

Chardra tracked it as it flew towards her and in the moment before they met, saw the tilt of its body, the steadying beat of its wings as it pushed its opened talons towards her, ready to pierce her body. She moved forward in a controlled tumble and pulled out her remaining knife.

There were no vantage points here. No highs or lows in the meadow's terrain, nor vegetation to use as a barrier or shield. She crouched and watched as the bird's talons closed on air. It screeched in anger at the miss. It pushed higher and then turned, wings brought in close to its body as it dove towards her.

Again, she waited. Just as it was a breath away from striking, she leaped to the side. Her arm swung wide, and her knife found its mark as it scored the Devourer's left-wing.

This time, its cry was one of anger and pain. Its landing was off balance and Chardra did not hesitate. With a massive show of strength and agility, she leaped forward and onto the creature's back. She plunged the knife into the bird time and time again, her legs clamped around its neck as if she was riding a beast of burden from the South.

The bird's hide was thick, and its feathers were sharp. Despite the hide leggings she wore, her flesh was cut and the tanned leather was turning an ugly black. Chardra dismissed the pain and focused only on delivering the killing blow.

The Devourer turned and hopped back and forth. It twisted its head, trying to peck at her body, but could not dislodge its prey. With no other choice, it spread its wings and tried to take flight. The injury to the left flight feathers was not enough to stop it from lifting its body a few feet off the ground.

Chardra knew if the Devourer were able to ascend much higher, her fight would be over. There were too many variables for her to hold her own against such a tactic. With all she had left, she grabbed the hilt of the knife with both hands, raised it above her head, and drove it down into the Devourer.

Its body shook from the impact, and Chardra pushed and pulled and ripped until her hands were soaked in blood and gore. The Devourer faltered, its body twisted and plummeted to the earth. Together they crashed into the meadow's embrace, tumbling over each other until both bodies became still.

There was life yet within the Devourer. Chardra pushed at the wing which had extended and covered her. As she freed herself, the Devourer shifted and its beak raked her back. She screamed at the burst of pain and fell forward to her knees.

With her knife buried in the back of the Devourer, all she could do was stagger to her feet and turn to face her opponent. A large bloodshot eye watched her and then blinked. Its body shifted in the grass, staining it red with its blood. Its beak opened in weak defiance, but it did not move again.

Chardra limped forward and stretched against the pain to wrench her knife free. Her hands slipped, slick with blood, and she fell backward. She cried out in pain and rolled onto her side. White-hot tears streaked down her cheeks as she forced herself to her feet once more. Again she stretched, teeth gritted, and pulled on the knife. With one last burst of strength, she wrenched it free from the Devourer's flesh.

Sobbing now, she staggered around the bird and fell inches away from its beak. If there was any life left in the great bird, now was its time to strike and deliver a killing blow.

It did not come.

Chardra leaned forward and parted the feathers on its brow. Hidden beneath its dark wings was a small protuberance, a piece of the Bone Tree. She took the edge of her knife's blade and pried it loose from its host. A foul-smelling liquid seeped out of the wound and Chardra turned and gagged.

As the stench dissipated, Chardra opened her hand and stared at the bone-white piece of wood. It was rough, with a long score mark down its side. Yet when the moonlight danced along its surface, flickers of light flared to life inside of it.

Eli's life force.

Her mind numb to the pain, she pushed herself up and made her way to the Bone Tree. The edges of Eli's skeleton were being wrapped in the tree's bark, pieces of his leg bones and ribs already absorbed into the ancient sentinel.

"No," she whispered. She could not be too late. She took the Bone Tree piece and touched it to Eli's skull, to the spot where the Devourer had touched him with its beak.

Her heart beat once…

…twice…

…and a third time…

The wood burned against her skin. Startled, she yanked her hand back. The piece remained affixed to Eli's skull as light pulsed from within. She took a step back, mesmerized as the light grew and wrapped itself around his body. Muscle and tendon grew and stretched. Skin wrapped itself around his body until Chardra cried out in relief as his eyelids fluttered open and his gaze found hers.

In her joy at seeing his body renewed, she missed how his legs and torso were not free of the Bone Tree. She stepped closer and touched her forehead to his.

"I should have listened," she sobbed.

"It would not have changed the currents," was his soft reply.

His hand reached out and ran down her cheek, and she shivered at the coldness of his touch.

"Eli?"

"There is nothing to fear. Nothing to mourn. The Upright foresaw the current you were meant to partake of. I was merely one possible channel for you to follow."

"I do not understand." Chardra pulled back, confusion written on her face, as she wiped at her tears.

"The Devourer and its ilk were blights upon the Heart of the Forest. Stealing what was not theirs to take and hiding that which belongs to all. The forest has longed for one to free it of its cage."

"I am not a Keeper, I am not trained in these things as you are."

"I know," Eli whispered as his hand slipped from her face. Chardra frowned and traced its fall, finally noting how his body was not free of the Bone Tree.

"No. I returned your life force to you." The words tumbled from her.

"You must listen. There is little time." Eli reached out and grabbed her hand in his. His ice-cold fingers burned her blood-slicked skin. "The Keepers know and understand what is to come. This is the night of Ethwam. The reshaping of our world into another. Return to the village. They will guide you as they can. In time, another will come who has been foretold by the Upright. One who will lead our people."

"I will not leave you." The words were fierce and true. Chardra leaned forward and kissed Eli. For a moment, the world stood still as each embraced the other until she could feel the life draining from him. "No, you cannot leave me."

"This is as the current wills it. Do not weep. Rejoice in what the Heart is to give."

"No!" Chardra could do nothing to stop Eli's eyelids from slipping closed, and his body sunk into the Bone Tree.

The moonlight hit the tree like lightning. Blue light raced up and down its crusted bark. Chardra stumbled back, mute, mind numb to what was happening in front of her.

The light intensified, burrowing through the Bone Tree's bark, from its roots to the tips of its outstretched branches, until the entire tree was glowing an unearthly blue. Moonlight filled the meadow and the Bone Tree's shadow grew until the light reflected the image of what it once had been. The shadow wavered, and the Bone Tree burst into a thousand glistening stars, riding the back of the wind and spreading its splinters throughout the forest.

Chardra winced as pieces of the Bone Tree pierced her skin and pushed their way inside of her. There was no pain in this, only a dulled sense of wonder as the light danced beneath her flesh.

"She is to be the first."

She whirled around. Her heart leaped at the sound of Eli's voice. But there was no one there. Only the meadow reflecting the twinkling stars of the night sky as the words echoed around her.

"She is to be the first."

"She is to be..."

"She is…"

A chill ran down her spine.

This was a story she did not yet understand.

Limping, she crossed the meadow, ignoring the playful breeze which followed her. The forest's shadows embraced her as she began the long journey back to her village. In the pain and weariness that crept into her body, she missed the sparks of light that winked as she passed. The forest was changing. As was she. Chardra did not yet understand the Huntress had died with her lover. She was returning to her people, not as she once had been, but as the Bone Woman she would become.

When it comes to the question of what sort of wings one might enjoy having, Tracy Eire finds value in many different types. But she's not opposed to albatross wings, for the albatross is known for flying through fierce winds and is able to circle the world in under fifty days. Intelligent, they use the winds to their advantage and draw upon internal energy to accomplish such feats.

Tracy's story also contains great energy, the rapid, brilliant notes of a violin played by character who leans into the wind and uses it to her own advantage

I HAVE A DEADLY NIGHTSHADE

Tracy Eire

CHLOE HAD CONTINUED TO DO the same things that were common in her life, which chiefly revolved around her post secondary school, L 'école des Cordes, her uncle's restaurant, and her parents' modest home, and yet something about her had *changed*.

She still liked math and science. She still hated mandatory courses in Voice. And, like clockwork every day, Chloe completed mathematics questions, sent them to her teacher through the classroom's network, only to tug the edge of some composition out from under her keyboard. Only in weekly gym couldn't she find a way to squirrel sheet music into, or underneath, something, only to draw it out again when she was unmonitored.

For her, *music never stopped*. It never stood still. When she woke up at night to head to her washroom, music was already playing in her brain, and it just rose to meet her in crescendo, to say *Hi. I'm here.* Her fingers flicked. Her hands curled around pencils, pens, and drinking straws like they were violin bows.

She woke up late on the day of the *violin solos.* Chloe was dimly aware of the morning sun that washed over where she listened to birds. Drifting in and out, lazing in the golden glow meant she had no time to wash her hair before she tore out of her house to get to school that day. It was put it up and run.

Because today was the day Maestro would choose lead violins!

So, Chloe Barin blew into L 'école des Cordes like a Simoom wind, a dusty tempest in the morning heat. She fell into the last remaining chair among the first violins, still trying to adjust the little violet tie at the throat of her uniform. Her chest was heaving as the full ensemble of orchestra came to rights. She'd been the last in. Except for a single person.

Maestro Keng strode through the door with a final backward 'thank you' to some administrator in the hallway beyond and crossed to his lectern. He didn't have a desk and didn't seem to miss it. He only ever carried two things, a folder or two full of sheet music for the day, and a baton he set on the lectern and then never seemed to use.

As usual, he stood in consideration of the folder he'd opened for a moment as the orchestra fell silent, its own seats in an arc around where he stood at the front of the room. Maestro Keng, quite apart from having his peers' respect, was admired by the students, and Chloe was sure it had *nothing* to do with the fact he looked like he'd aged out of a Korean Boy

Band a few months prior, only to reveal heretofore unappreciated abilities in classical and jazz music direction.

Sure.

She stared at him a little agog and hoped that someday someone like him would be in her future, because Chloe couldn't *imagine* wanting to date a boy who wasn't a musician. Well, not then anyway. A few seconds more, and Maestro Keng nodded.

He glanced up from the lectern and smiled, "Afternoon."

The tension broke into, "Welcome, Maestro."

The full orchestra was gathered, none of them wanted to miss this day, and made the reply quite a cacophony in the acoustical room.

He went to the little closet, opened the wood door, and took out a folding chair. It was padded and red, like all the chairs around them, but covetous 16-year-old eyes followed it as he walked it back to the front of the spacious classroom. He unfolded and tucked it into the space closest to his lectern. Then dusted off his hands and grinned, "Cold."

The metal was cold, Chloe understood from that. The chair had been in storage till now.

The orchestra around her burbled with amusement, apart from many of the violins, whose emotions didn't allow for frivolity right then. Chloe, for all her bravado and new-found confidence, for all her changes, felt nearly queasy. She turned her head and arranged her dark brown hair so that she couldn't see the new chair sitting there, even if she could still sense it *calling* to her underneath it all, like a D string plucked on an upright bass: *bung. Bung. Bung.*

Go away. She tried to hush it. Or maybe that was her heartbeat?

With four people in the running, this wasn't going to be easy. Or even *possible.*

But Chloe, who'd started orchestra a bit behind, was most improved of them all.

She clung doggedly to that.

Maestro Keng nodded at them. "For those new to the concept, today is the day I will begin selection of a lead violin. It's quite a tough decision to make of our talent, especially this year."

"He says that *every time,*" whispered a young man behind Chloe.

Chloe tried to ignore this little aside. She sat beside their section today, and *everyone* knew the woodwinds were *terrible* gossips.

Maestro Keng patted the lectern before him with the back of his hand, his knuckles making soft pops off the wood. "We've separated players into first and second violins, but today, I will announce the final three violinists in the running for a position known as Concertmaster. As you know, a good Concertmaster is critical not just to the coordination of the violin section, but the entire orchestra. They lead the orchestra in tuning for concerts. So, you will be looking to the violin selected for *leadership.*"

Heads turned among the violins, and, doubtless, the rest of the orchestra.

The Maestro shut and held up a folder. "We'll play in unison because of their work. They will lead smaller ensembles. I will be marking the score according to their bowing. The Concertmaster will sit to one side of this podium," he double-tapped the lectern with the folder, "because the chosen violinist will solo whenever needed. The Concertmaster, or first chair, is *critical* to the success of our orchestra. It's a big job, and a quite serious pursuit."

He stepped back and set down the folder. "Auditions begin tomorrow. I will hand out sheets with pieces from our former performances, and general requirements for each of you. Let's see how you play *in situ*, with a night to brush up." The Maestro rubbed his hands together. "All right. The orchestra and I will give you five beats. Violinists auditioning for first chair... stand now." He opened his flattened hands in air. The ensemble did the same.

When Maestro clapped his hands, the whole orchestra did the same, almost in time.

One clap rolled in the room.

Two.

Did she really want to do this?

Chloe listened to the noise around her. Could she handle the pressure? The responsibility? Could she manage the solos and tunings and Maestro marking the score to the bob of her bow tip?

Three.

It was only when she realized she was smiling that she knew that though she was nervous, she was also excited.

Four.

Eyes closed, she stood up.

Five.

Silence.

I did it.

She opened her eyes again. Cheers and applause broke out among the orchestra.

Maestro called out, "Come to the front please."

Chloe soon found herself standing with violinists who were widely considered the school's best. There was Momo Agawa, who was almost six feet tall, rail thin, who attacked pieces with the intensity of a runway model. She practiced three hours every night, religiously. Kendrick Mackey was fiendishly fast and so skilled he'd been teaching others lately. Carnelia Ball was a quick learner, solid at everything she was asked to do, and had won six prizes and awards away from the orchestra, doing solos. And there *she* stood: *Chloe Barin. Most improved. Most changed.* The others were a mix of emotions from stunned to annoyed by her presence.

It was her first moment of misgiving. She stared down at her scuffed UGGs and then up at the Maestro. He raised his chin, and she followed suit. Of all of them, he seemed unsurprised by the line-up here. "Let's give all of our candidates a hand."

There was a final round of applause, which carried on while Maestro passed each of them sheet music from the second folder on his desk. At the time, Chloe was so excited to be counted among these players that she didn't even read it.

I SAID NO PICKLES." CHLOE paused in the smell of greasy fried foods and glanced back at the man who sat along the long white counter. He dwarfed the cap of the diner's stool, huge, bearded, and pugnacious. The bill of his red baseball hat bobbed as he noted. "No. Pickles."

"Oh, I didn't know."

"How? I gave you my order," he snapped.

"No, sir. You gave my sister your order. I'm working the..." but it was probably useless to explain the table assignments to a guy like this one.

"Yeah, well you look alike."

Chloe didn't know what to say to that. They *were* related.

He showed her the plate. "Let's see if you can follow here. *What are those*?" He pointed at the green pair of slices of house pickles. Her uncle liked to use them to decorate the plate and 'give the dish a pop of acid'.

"A side of pickles," Chloe said in defeat.

"Then *fix it*." He threw up a hand at her. "I said *no* God damn pickles. Get me my money back."

She scooped up the order. "I'll tell the cook." Chloe peeled to one side and hurried down the narrow hall toward the kitchen.

"Hey! Why are you takin' that? You're *not* getting a tip!" He shouted after her.

What a huge surprise that is. She pushed through the doors and into the bright white kitchen. There was her mother dipping blueberry perogies from a pot. She up-ended the load of them onto a cloth to soak out excess grease, and then slid them along the counter. Her uncle, set a final basket of deep-fried matzo and veggie balls at the pass, and called. "Service."

"What are you doing back here, honey?" Chloe's mother caught sight of her through the steam and motion in the kitchen.

"Lemme catch you up, mom. Elijah put *pickles* on an order with *No Pickles. I* look like *Michelle.* Seat 2 wants a free sandwich *and* a refund." Chloe ducked out the open back door and hurried down the steps to a teenaged guy in worn jeans and a hoodie who appeared to be *hanging out* in the alley. She handed over the order to the grateful teen before she hurried back inside.

It was Elijah's place, and he didn't waste untouched food.

"Is he being a jerk, *ahuva*?" Her father called from the vegetable station as she re-entered.

"Yeah, dad." Chloe admitted. "I'm going to steer Michelle clear of him."

"Jake, go give that guy a refund?" Her father asked.

Elijah glanced away from the Kegul balls he was carefully dolloping with house sauce and nudged Jake, the only one in the room neither doing something with food, nor moving at all. "Jake, wake up! A customer's giving your sisters a hard time and trying to scam a meal! Seat 2."

"Come on son." Her dad gave Jake a push that woke him with a snort, and he got to his feet. "Seat 2 needs a refund. He's insulted your sister."

"Which one?" Jake sounded sleepily annoyed.

"I think both of them," said Elijah. He barely paid attention to Jake, who probably could have lifted a freezer on his own, as he grumbled by.

Michelle came out of the staff room, drying her hands, "Is the redneck gonna feel the heat of waking Jake from his nap, or what?" But her eyes were red at the rims.

Chloe stopped. "Did that bozo make you *cry*?"

Her younger sister's brows drew up at the bridge of her nose, and she shrugged, having failed to hide it. Off to Chloe's right, her mother dumped out perogies and wiped her hands in the towel over one shoulder. She passed her ladle to her sister-in-law and crossed the rectangle of kitchen, navigating around the rolling island, to hug her 14-year-old daughter.

This only made Michelle cry harder, and Chloe felt her back stiffen. "Mom… tell Michelle to go upstairs and take the night off."

"Honey, she wants to help out," said her father.

"Maybe not when it's busy, okay?" Chloe washed her hands again and ducked to find a clean terry towel for herself. She mumbled, "Not that you can *help* a total *ass* like that guy."

The bump beside her as she finished with the towel was… Michelle.

"Go upstairs," Chloe told her younger sister.

"Nope," said the other girl, determinedly. She swung a hand to point across the kitchen at the 8-peg wooden coat rack mounted by the work schedules.

"I know, you put your name down for this shift, but I'm your older sister. You have to listen to me." Chloe tugged the ties of her apron and started for the door. "Go upstairs."

Michelle cut in front of her. "No." She pointed again, and this time… Chloe stopped.

Her little sister wasn't waving at the schedule. There, hung on the pegs over her coat was her violin case. She glanced back at Michelle's determined face. "My violin?"

"You can't work all the evening shifts anymore, Chloe." Michelle's finger stabbed at the violin, and she swept by her older sister with, "I'm okay, mom. You worry too much."

Maybe for the first time that night, Chloe took a deep breath and stood still. A moment later, Elijah nudged her. "You gonna go do the thing?"

Her eyes were embarrassingly damp as she nodded Yes.

"You're a bright kid," Elijah said. "But Michelle's got her own mind too. Now head outside."

Minutes later, Chloe stood on the back ramp of the alley with sheet music pinned down on a clipboard hung from the back door on a string. There were people laughing as they walked the busy downtown, and the puffs of steam like smoke signals spiralled up from friers next door. A car nearly had a fender-bender in the traffic beyond her, and two grown men started arguing. But once the first bittersweet slow notes of Sibelius Violin Concerto in D minor rose from the body of her violin and spiralled up into the night, Chloe was transported.

Some part of her departed the planet, and the only strings that tied her to earth were those of her precious instrument.

Usually, she could practice an hour, or maybe two out here, but no one came for her for close to four hours that night. She was exhausted when her mother pulled her indoors again. "Come on, Chloe. It's time for you to head upstairs to sleep."

"Was there a noise complaint, mom?" Chloe asked in exhaustion.

Michelle, who beamed at her from the sink exclaimed, "*Who cares*?! That was beautiful!"

"No, honey." Her mother locked and barred the back door, pulled the curtains, and then turned to her. "For that, you'd have to be making *noise*."

Her music wasn't a *racket*. Not at all. They smiled at each other.

"Go to bed, honey," Chloe's mother said. "Big day tomorrow."

IT RAINED ON THE DAY they played the first audition.

At 3:05, after the rest of school had let out, Chloe stood in her assigned classroom with her violin in hand and walked through the requirements *mentally*. She didn't play a note though the music of others filled the room. She didn't consider the piece the candidates would be playing to be terribly difficult, but rather a solid piece of her current repertoire, and she was grateful for all the hours she'd spent playing it *slllooowwwly*. The requirements were… harder. She did focus on those.

But there was such a thing as overdoing it.

She stood with one hand on her violin case drumming out a beat, and tapping her heel, to enjoy the hard rain along a third-floor row of windows. Finally, she turned in place and snatched up a pencil from the teacher's desk which she held in air to conduct. Chloe had no realistic idea what really went into that, so she simply did her best imitation of how Maestro worked when directing them. With a couple of little waggles she pretended were *signature Maestra Barin.*

The door tapped and Chloe turned quickly and flung the pencil through air and onto the floor.

The little wood and graphite tube was still making its high woody sound as the door opened a crack and Kendrick Mackey glanced in. "Hi Chloe."

"Hi Kendrick." She said a little tightly. *I was being normal. Totally normal.*

He nodded, "Uh, we're all a classroom or so apart up here. If you didn't know."

"Yeah. I can hear." She nodded at this. "Is something wrong?"

"You're just... I'm in the classroom up from you and it's really quiet down here. I was starting to worry you were backing out," he confessed. His hand swept up to smooth the curls of his hair. "Are you?"

"*No folding,*" she said without thinking.

"Yeah," he smiled. "You're pretty resilient."

Chloe shrugged, "You want to come in? Some people feel more pressure if they're alone."

"Are you that person?" He stepped inside with his violin case.

"Sometimes," she admitted to him. "But I'm keeping myself entertained."

He set down his violin and sat in the teacher's chair a moment before he said, "*So weird.*"

She laughed at this as she put her hair back. "I wouldn't even go there, so *yay* for you."

He sighed and rubbed at the chest of his jacket-front. "Are you worried about anyone?"

"I... hadn't given it any thought," she admitted. "You?"

Now Kendrick turned to peer out at the sheeting rain and slate grey sky. "Are you... like did you know that Momo Agawa's violin cost 20,000 dollars?"

Now Chloe's eyes widened, and she stopped still. "What?"

"Yeah." He tapped his case. "So, I don't know if you've been introduced, but this is my violin Clive, like for the playwright? This is a 950-dollar violin, but it's... it's like a fiddle compared to even that purplish abomination of Carnelia's. That thing cost almost 9000 dollars. Like, can you even imagine how amazing those violins sound? My poor Clive! Up against those beasts! It's like David and Goliath." He picked up the violin and held it close for a moment.

"Carnelia's violin cost," Chloe drew out the words, "*9000-dollars.*"

"And Momo's was *20 large.* She told me she named it *Peachy.*" Kendrick nodded up at her. "How scary is that?"

Well, it was *terrifying.* She pressed a hand to the lump forming in her throat.

She had to shake herself back to reality, drag her gaze off the battered case and its duct-taped corner. It had been... 500-dollars second hand. She loved her violin. But what kind of tone could it produce to compare with Momo's 'Peachy'?

"Hey," Kendrick said, "How are we going to know to go to audition? There was no other time than standard practice written on my sheet. I double checked it."

"Mine either." She glanced around. "I'm tuning and waiting."

Well, Chloe's mother had hugged her warmly in the morning, and her dad had given her a peck on the cheek for luck. Michelle had crossed her fingers on the way to her friends on the school bus, and Jake had applauded her from his upstairs window.

That, and a 500-dollar violin was what she had.

"Hold it? Do you hear something?" Kendrick looked up at Chloe.

Then he got up, took his violin and case, and crossed to the door and to... rising music?

Chloe checked her watch. 3:30 PM. She glanced if Kendrick was looking, and then stroked her violin case one-handed. *I don't care about the others. My parents saved to get you, so their hearts are in every note. Plus, I think that makes you family.*

She picked up her case, her ponytail swinging as she headed along the whiteboards toward the doorway. Kendrick had been right. Violins played nearby. Why was that?

She went into the hall and found all the candidates had left their rooms. It sounded like violin warm up outside... but loud and approaching. As she trotted down the hallway the chaos turned into a sudden rest, and...?

Luigi Boccherini's Minuet, in tempo. It sounded so refined. The staircase, when she reached it, was full of violin students arrayed on the landings, playing. When they saw her, they smiled, which helped Chloe's flagging courage. How many of them had 8- and 20,000-dollar violins, after all? And the music sounded divine. She followed Momo, Kendrick, and Carnelia down the staircase and around the corner to the music room. The rest of the violins piled in after them, a jumble of excited conversations.

From the front of the room, Chloe set down her battered violin case to applaud them and the other candidates joined in.

Maestro Keng was pleased with this, that much was clear. "Well done," he said into the silence that fell. "For today, you'll be playing a mixture of works we've practiced throughout your time in the orchestra, as I suggested on the sheet, you should have brushed up last night. I would like to see your retention. I'll also want to go through fundamentals with you, and for that, we'll be using a true classic."

Everyone waited nearly breathless in the tapping of rain.

And Maestro Keng said, "The Sleeping Beauty Waltz. Tchaikovsky."

Kendrick and Momo might have chuckled, but what followed was a dizzying, even gruelling 20 minutes of rapid switches between violin techniques and pieces. Chords, double stops, double stop glissandos, tenths, the list went on with Maestro leaning in to observe, and to call out the next switch. Chloe had to accept what she didn't do cleanly and forge ahead. Momo clucked her tongue aloud and paused as her brain vapour-locked at one point. Kendrick bared his teeth against the rapid shift into trills versus notes, one of each, every other note. Brisk allegro switched to even faster presto then down Tempo again. It had some of the orchestra laughing, until everyone saw how difficult it was as a purely technical exercise. In the end, only Chloe and Carnelia made it through that part of testing.

Maestro's hands stayed in motion to direct them.

He brought their volume down low, like the fade of a song.

But then he sent them straight into etudes with no break. The Maestro's hands moved smoothly, "Mendelsshon, Violin Concerto in E Minor." The selection of etudes was the second half of the technical section, or so her worksheet had said. She'd made it this far. This part of the testing operated—as far as Chloe could discern—like an IQ test. Namely, pieces kept getting harder and harder, until the players tapped out, or had three strikes.

So far, Momo had sat down. Her head drooped over her gorgeous violin like a lily so that they were an excellent synergy, those two—heartbreaking for Chloe to witness. Kendrick fell out next, visibly angry he'd racked up three strikes during a shift that Chloe and Carnelia threw both their torsos into.

Which was when Chloe felt herself beginning to tighten up, her fingertips pressed strings to the violin's fingerboard *far* too hard. She began to worry *What next?* Would her shoulders become taut? No, her elbows would stiffen first. Would her wrist lose its flex next? Or would it be the buttery smoothness of her fingers that seized up and betrayed?

Strings worked player while in down-bow, or pizzicato, while their fingers searched for 7th position, by playing out the musician's tension, their anxiety, and their confidence. It wasn't a one-way street.

She pulled in air and steadied. She was changed now.

The practice, the commitment. Something was different inside. Something she could trust.

Her body began to return itself to its state of ease. Her joints flexed, her muscles glided, and her fingertips pressed only enough to make the purest of tones. She wondered if anyone could detect the difference this second wind made. Almost as soon as she thought that, the Maestro tapped his earlobe and flicked up a finger. But to *Carnelia*. It was the first strike either of them, the final two players, had had. Chloe felt herself breathing harder but mastered her anxiety. She gathered it close like a tumble of ducklings. *Keep warm. Keep calm. Grow.*

She got her first strike on Paganini Violin Concerto No. 1 in D Major. *No surprise there.* She hadn't put enough time into it yet. She needed more practice. But Chloe had gotten close to 30 seconds to herself with the piece before that happened.

Maestro closed his hands. "You're a bit slow on the Paganini, Miss Barin. Not a bad choice here."

The room was quiet as Chloe had to reach up and daub her temples. She was *sweating.*

Applause followed as the weight of expectation in the room burst and the orchestra unloaded their admiration on the four candidates.

During that moment, Chloe glanced down at her 500-dollar violin and felt happiness.

Nice work, munchkin.

"Miss Barin, exceptional." Said the Maestro, who looked a mixture of proud and excited with this students' advancements. "Take a bow all of you. There will be some recovery and practice time allotted before the final audition. For now, *brava! Bravo!*"

"*Thank you.*" Carnelia's eyes widened, "Hm. I think I pulled a muscle."

Chloe laughed at this, which got her a sharply amused look from red headed Carnelia.

A group of 16-years-old passing through this nonstop testing? Ploughing through etudes and *Paganini*?

When Chloe straightened again, even Maestro Keng was applauding.

No wonder he was proud.

AS SHE BUSTLED AROUND THE grand old school and its green campus, sat practicing in her cubicle of bedroom, or worked off nervous energy at her uncle's restaurant, Chloe felt a growing certainty, she couldn't quite describe.

She would overhear snippets of conversation in the hallways of L 'école des Cordes like:

Any idea what they'll be playing for final audition?
That's one of the four strings now—right there!
There's a delay in choosing the concertmaster, I heard.
Well, there hasn't been a race for first chair like this in years.

But, for the most part, the intervening week was average for Chloe. In that simple way of 16-year-old girls coming into their own power she'd fallen in love, and love had made her blind. Still, it was understandable. What forces in their lives ever urged young women onto their own paths? What powers lay in moonlit pillows beside their foreheads and whispered about charting their dreams beside the great constellations? However, Chloe Barin had begun to have those conversations with herself. Sometimes, there was precious little between her and legend, just a rail no thicker than a bow stick that she could feel in the dark, leading up, when so many young women were taught that their entire value lay in giving up everything, so someone else could dream.

And... she wondered as she pulled a chamois cloth over the violin that had gotten her here, what was the delay in choosing a Concertmaster about, anyway? She buried her frustration in checking and rechecking, held the violin aloft between her chin and shoulder rest and reached up along it to turn a fine tuner on her D string.

Practice had just broken up for the day. But fussing and wiping down her violin at the end of class was a ritual of Chloe's. There was an oboe who would stay and play a pure A note as classes let out so that she could tune. That Thursday, he smiled and carried his case over in Chloe's direction, but was cut off when Carnelia hurried through the room and over to her.

"Chloe-Chloe-Chloe!" The red head said excitedly. She was dynamic, with a lively personality, Carnelia. "Do you have any plans for the weekend?"

"What? Me?" Chloe set her bow in her case, took off her shoulder rest, and started to put her violin away, not sure what to say. It turned out she didn't need to say anything at all.

Carnelia held up two envelops she waggled in air. "You do now!"

She handed one to Chloe.

"What's... this?" Chloe asked even as she was unfolding it.

"The music list for final audition! I just came from Maestro's office!" Carnelia waved her own at Chloe and danced in place a little before she opened it up. The oboe had given up by then and left the excited girls some of the last in the orchestral room. So, dancing up and down was legitimate.

"Wednesday 4 PM," Chloe flapped a hand at herself. "Oh my gosh!"

"Yeah, finally." Carnelia made a little squeak of delight and shook out her red curls. "What about the music list?"

Chloe stared at it and, though Carnelia stood beside her, her own letter up so that she could dab her fingertips at titles and chatter, Chloe had a moment of consternation.

She could... play better than this list.

That was no slight at all to the music, and certainly not to the composers, but L 'école des Cordes was an East Coast alternative to Juilliard, post one scandalous exposé after another. The millionaire faculty members and billion-dollar endowments translated into unsanitary conditions, yearly fees of nearly 80,000 dollars and rising, and aging facilities that were never updated. The media had made meals out of fire-code violations like locking protesting students in rooms and halls, and crafting rules that ensured anyone who complained was banned from the premises and couldn't avoid an incomplete on their transcripts.

Juilliard big boys had ensured no musician could voice a complaint and matriculate. Convenient. And *utterly corrupt*. All had been well for them until the outraged faculty had voted with their wing tips. L 'école des Cordes had been born. The old school was a smaller pond, for certain, but all the fish in it grew big and thrived like koi. And it, fuelled by the resources that had made Juilliard *worthwhile*—the staff—was *better* than the collection of songs in her hand now.

Chloe walked out into the hallway with Carnelia, just trying to make sense of this inconsistency.

She almost ploughed directly into Momo Agawa.

Momo's downcast face was drawn where she went up the hallway, violin swinging at her shoulder, in a waft of Chanel and fineries as her parents swept by with her.

She gave both girls a doleful eye.

Up the hall, Maestro was standing with the Headmistress of L'école, the esteemed Simone Zhang. Several of the staff ambled as they waited and appeared grave as Momo and her wealthy family approached.

"What's going on?" Chloe stopped to ask.

"Oh my gosh," Carnelia's eyes were wide. One pale-nailed hand swept up to her lips. "Momo looks *miserable*. Do you think she's in trouble?"

Chloe raised her audition worksheet to wave at Maestro and his head, tight with tension, gave a small nod. "*Why* would she be in trouble?"

"Because her dad is Atsu Agawa, the *conductor*, Chloe. Seriously." Carnelia winced across at her. "And she was the first of us to strike out of the technical test."

This made Chloe forget song choice and straighten up in disbelief. She turned to Carnelia. "You don't think her parents *blame* her? Do you?"

"I don't know them." Carnelia looked momentarily dumbfounded. "But I think... I can guess why the final has been delayed. Maestro Agawa would've had to fly in from London for this."

"*London?*" Chloe repeated in astonishment.

"If you can believe it. For this conversation." Carnelia glanced at her after the doors at the end of the hall sucked in all the professors, Momo, and the storied conductor. Both girls were drawn.

And that was how they parted ways.

She was still dazed as she passed the car that came to pick up Kendrick every day. He glanced across at her and grinned, "Lots of luck with your music selection, Chloe."

She glanced across at him. "Were you here when Momo came through?"

He nodded gravely. "Yeah, I saw."

Chloe squinted up at the windows of the school, "Okay, you too. Kendrick. See you next week."

He tucked into the car with his violin, and Chloe sat on the bus and stared at the sheet of music selections. But no matter what she did, she couldn't come to terms with it.

IT WASN'T REALLY POSSIBLE TO practice properly at home, which meant, bright and early, she and the list were on the first bus to her local theatre. It was about 12 blocks from *Nosh,* the restaurant her family had opened just a couple of years back now. If the Barin's were bold enough for that, Chloe was bold enough to ask for places to play and practice.

And that's what the local theatre and performance hall, small as it was, had become. The bus stopped right in front of the building, and she caught her violin case up and headed eagerly through open gates. It was dusty and in constant renovation, this big wooden building, but the owner let her practice in the loft for free.

Now, many of the theatre kids were friends.

"Hey Chloe." One of the young men with a blue paintbrush in hand hailed her. The pong of acrylic wafted to her as she paused on the steps. He was painting a set on a drop-cloth outside the theatre, and it was large enough that six other people were helping. They had created what looked like the Alps. He smiled, "Mendelssohn today? I hope?"

"Not sure yet." She waved and called back from the sunny concrete steps she climbed. "Are you doing *The Sound of Music*?"

He threw his hands up and laughed, "It's for *William Tell*! Why does everyone think it's *The Sound of Music*?"

The rest of the painters laughed, and one pointed her gray brush. "I'll pay you later, Chloe!"

She went smilingly into the shadow of the building, and through the wood doors. Everything inside was old, but serviceable. The plank floor had been painted white. The wood stairs creaked along windows so towering anyone on them was fully visible from the outside. She spiralled upward in the sun and could imagine her notes falling like fat golden raindrops, to splash on any upturned faces. And wouldn't they glitter with gold too?

The loft room had an enclosed space, walled in with long slats of bead board to gird it, and an open one—which she chose. It was as it always appeared, full of easels and art carts covered in drop cloth. It smelled of oil paint and medium up here, but mildly. Everything had to be safely stored and put away at the end of classes. The cloths kept dust off wet paintings as they dried. Or... so she'd been told. Each one draped in a rough triangle, out from the easel to cover the chair backs. Chloe always checked that none touched the canvases. She'd been told a careless touch could ruin a work.

At the front of the room was the tall wood podium kept for her.

At first, it had been rough, this stand. Then the theatre kids had sanded off the old blue paint. And a week or two later, the art students had stained and varnished it for her. To this day, it sometimes had the most amazing sketches of her playing violin set on it, though, not today. She looked back at the easels gratefully. She had memories like these, of the hall. Once, the power had gone, and she'd played in near darkness through a windstorm. Down on the stage a dozen flamenco dancers had practiced to her music by candlelight.

It had always been full of magic, this place.

One of the theatre buffs—Molly—tapped the door. "Chloe, we have lemonade. Want some?"

"Thanks." Chloe went to join them in the storage room down the hall. It was thick with dust and dryness inside the back room, and several people squatted by piles of books and lamps, and old furnishings, on the swept floor. Chloe recognized everyone as part of the University troupe that was always in the woodwork when she came here, but she'd never noticed this door before and marvelled, "I didn't even realize this was here. What are you doing?"

"The owner said *the key* was found during renovation," said the excited young man who had come to share lemonade. His grin flashed at her as he went to a table and poured her a cup from a pitcher full of ice. "That's not even the best part. When the contractors took down the old wainscot, that's when they found *the door*."

Chloe's found this astonishing. "This is a secret room?"

Another girl, who Chloe knew to be Molly, stood up and crossed to her. "And it's our job to catalog everything! Isn't it thrilling? And don't be thoughtless, Graeme! Chloe, want biscotti? I bet you came straight over and didn't have a bite to eat. There's yogurt."

"What are *you* talking about?" Chloe laughed. "It's 8 AM, and you all look like you've been here for hours!"

Graeme took out a scrubbed, but very clearly antique plate for her. He set her favourite biscotti on it—her sweet tooth no secret to her theatre friends. "Can you blame us?"

She was still smiling as she took the lemonade and biscotti back down the hall to prep for practice. Intermediate level music. "Gavotte from Mignon?" She sighed. "This can't be right. She decided to run through everything that had been written on the list, but then...? Chloe had a secret. That secret was how much she'd been practicing Paganini Violin Concerto No.1 and Sibelius Violin Concerto in D minor, the latter of which she could play end-to-end *exceptionally*. It was one of her *favourites*.

She was going to nail down her performance of Concerto No.1 next.

Her fingers itched for Sibelius, though. Just to warm up on the strings.

Chloe opened her violin case and a roll of magazines fell out.

She stood and stared. Still.

She looked at the collection of car and girly magazines on the floor beside her and howled like a knife had plunged into something vital.

She found herself on the floor just staring at the horrible roll of magazines.

"Chloe!" Theatre kids flooded in. Molly glanced over the case and magazines on the floor and frowned. "Where's the violin?"

But Chloe, whose brain was full of flaming fumes, didn't hear her.

"Mom?" She exhaled shakily into the phone she'd pulled up to her ear.

"Honey, what's wrong?" Her mother asked at once.

"Did you see my violin this morning?" Useless question since Chloe *knew* she'd packed it up before she'd gone to bed.

"No darling. I only heard you playing it last night?"

Chloe clapped a hand over her face. "Mom, it's gone."

In the world around her, Molly shot up. "Someone took her violin?"

Graeme gawked, "She was only with us *a few minutes.*"

"We should shut the doors." One of the other young women bounced up.

Students tore downstairs. The news spread across the theatre rapidly, doors were locked, set painters gave statements of everyone they'd seen coming and going, and Chloe tried to explain the loss of a 500-dollar instrument to a family who'd put everything they had into a restaurant.

Inside her, the stab wound bled.

The owner came upstairs only minutes after the event and stood by the passageway. The woman had come to see her secret room, but her eyes were full of young prodigy, Chloe Barin, crumpled on the floor of the loft as she sobbed to her mother over the phone.

She turned to her partner and exhaled, "Call the police."

The officers arrived to take Chloe's statement some 15 minutes later.

"And these aren't your magazines?" Asked one as he glanced through the porn.

The owner looked aside at him sharply and the question didn't come up again.

In all that time, Chloe had yet to get up from the floor where she'd fallen. She didn't feel capable of turning to look at her empty violin case.

In the end, Molly collected the case *and* the girl, and brought them into the next room. Pinched and breathless as she was, Chloe was recovering. "My mom said she'd come when her shift ended, but Nosh is short handed tonight. Even my brother is working."

"I thought he was useless and pretty?" Graeme noted. "Didn't you say that to me once?"

"I was being a jerk." Chloe cracked a smile and rubbed an eye.

Molly threw an arm around her waist, "*Big brothers*, right? Sit with us until she gets here."

"I mean, when did you last see it?" Graeme asked as she settled down and shoved some biscotti into her cheek.

"I practiced last night." She shook her head.

"Then you left the house with it." Molly nipped her lip. "Did you bus here like usual?"

"Yeah." Chloe exhaled. "I... can use a spare at school. It's just... lower quality. I have till Wednesday to get used to the feel, and a new bow." She wiped a cheek. A whole new instrument just in time for the biggest audition of her life, so far? Success would be *impossible*.

The theatre students exchanged unhappy glances of agreement at that.

"It's been stolen by some *idiot*." Graeme said resentfully. "Either they were on the bus with you, or they knew you came here, and they took it while we showed you the room."

"It's not your fault," Chloe's voice broke. She opened her arms at the vagary of chance. Part of her was missing. It was out there flying through the world without her, and no one loved it out there.

The owner ducked into the room. Ms. Chang was as stoic as she'd ever been, but there was something underlying that composure now. "Are you doing okay?"

"I am. I'm sorry for the... dramatics," Chloe apologized. "I have an audition for first chair at L 'école des Cordes on Wednesday. I'll have time to find a replacement... and get used to it."

"Don't apologize, dear." Ms. Chang told her. "Call me when the police get back in touch." She headed out, presumably downstairs to her office.

"What's a first chair?" Molly asked her, finally.

"That's the violin—the *person*—who leads the orchestra." Chloe clarified. "I'm one of four people in the running. Everyone's been calling us *the 4 strings*, like on a violin, G, D, A, E. Like that. And they've been saying there hasn't been a competition like this one in-"

She stopped short. Got up and opened her case.

"What is it?" Molly asked.

Chloe searched the few contents. The zipper pouch held gum, her bus pass, and her undisturbed wallet with 60 bucks and School ID in it. She sat back on her heels a moment, left it open, and went into the loft room. But try as she might... there was no sign of it.

"What?" Molly opened her arms in exasperation.

"They stole my violin...."

"That we established," Graeme leaned on the doorframe.

"And my bow." Her hand rose up as if she held it. She took in the mournful, stressed faces of the pair and realized that they really did care about her. Chloe's head cocked. "They knew enough about violins to do that... but they also took my *audition worksheet*."

"What's that?" Molly shrugged.

"L 'école des Cordes gives musicians worksheets for auditions. They took my *worksheet*. It was folded under the violin, but it has no value."

She got up and passed through the wood-scented hall to the secret room. There she could show them that the inside of the violin case was designed with raised, padded ridges, so that when the violin's back set on it, there was a space under and above it. Sure, the case had been dinged and taped up, but Chloe had kept it *because* it had been so well constructed.

"They left your wallet, all your money, but took some worksheet?" Graeme shook his head. "What?"

"That's just... senseless." Molly frowned.

It was *so odd*. Chloe could still remember the pieces that had been puzzling her.

And that left her with a suspicion inside, as if her mind had invited her to pick a card, any card, and behind it was sleight of hand done for her benefit.

"Are you okay?" Molly strode over, her dark skin and hair painted in orange-gold by the light of the setting sun. She stooped to help Chloe up to her feet again.

"Can... can I work with you guys for a while?" She glanced across at Graeme, whose grave nod presaged the answer. "Until my mother can come over?"

Molly gave her a quick hug, unbidden, which was warm and helpful. The girl smiled so widely her cheek pinched in around its piercing. "Chloe, you can work with us *any* time."

They cleared the room in one corner all the way to the back.

The sun was newly declined when Chloe stood with a lantern-flashlight at the back wall.

There stood a cobwebbed and dusty built-in case that ran floor to ceiling. She flicked it with the dust cloth she held in one hand, and covered her nose and mouth with the other, just as Molly had warned her to do.

"How is it going?" The owner, Ms. Chang, carried a package and another pair of battery-operated lanterns she set on the table runner. "Did you know there was a first edition Sherlock Holmes book in here? Marcus brought it to me. It's like we're working our way back to 1871 in this room. Oh, my gracious, the dust! Can we open a window yet?" The woman coughed.

"I can!" Chloe coughed back.

"Is that Chloe Barin still here helping us out?" Asked the owner.

"Yeah, it is." Molly smiled. "Are those *masks*?"

"I had spares."

Chloe could hear the rattle of packaging opening behind her, and she extended a hand to push at the window latch which she eventually worked free. Fresh spring air blew into the room, flushed the dust, and she eased back to stare at the moon rising. The windows here weren't large, but stout instead, and in a long strip. They really did look to be from another time.

She crouched and started opening the drawers on the large built in. They were sticky, but they moved with a little coaxing. "Boy you've got work ahead of you." The drawer was stuffed. She worked it open and shut again. Halfway up, Chloe froze.

She'd opened one long drawer and, sitting inside on a diagonal, was a dirty black violin case, coffin style. Her brain refused to accept the find. That was her first reaction.

Chloe walked out of the path they'd made to the drawers and stood looking at the 6 or so people, clustered around the owner as she placed a delivery order to thank them for their work.

"Your family owns a restaurant, don't they?" Graeme nodded at her and held up his phone. "Nosh, right? Do they deliver?"

Chloe set a hand over the quavering in her chest. "Uh. Yes. And... I'll call them for you if that would help you to-"

"Nonsense. We're adults," replied Ms. Chang. "I will go through the ordering system. What should I try?"

"Oh. The Chicken Paprikash is my favourite lately, and the uhm—given the situation—maybe you want to go with the Key Challah. Also, dessert perogies." She wiped an eyelid. "They're blueberry."

Ms. Chang's head rose, "So I shall. The food is my treat to you all for this work." She turned and went out into the hallway, "Is this Ms. Barin? Hm. I'm with your daughter at the Resource Centre for the Arts? She practices here...?"

Chloe remembered herself and made a grave nod of her head. "Molly? I think I found a violin."

The entire group of theatre buffs turned as one. Graeme's mouth hung open, "What are you waiting for, Chloe? What if it's *playable*?"

"I'm afraid to look." Chloe laid a hand on her stomach's nearly sickening knot of hope.

Molly wasn't the only one of them to hurry by her. Soon, the little hall down to the back was jammed full of theatre students. "It's got a case made of... I think it's wood? It's got..." Chloe heard the *ker-clatter* in the swirl of crisp spring air, "hook latches?"

When silence fell, she couldn't help but hurry down the little passageway again, push through people making way for her, to come to a stop by the window she'd opened. The moon had risen just enough that, as Molly stepped back, and Graeme leaned over her shoulder... the light fell across an unlatched wood case. "It's old." Chloe reached out and put her hands on the wood in the blue moonlight and lifted it out to lay across the drawer. No one spoke.

Three beats later—she could almost hear the orchestra clapping— she opened it.

The rise of gasps and one high whistle of admiration brought her back from prayers.

The case had a full-sized violin and a bow inside. The violin's reddish gold wood stain appeared almost... hand rubbed into its surface. An ornate metal name plate sat on a little drawer that had once held rosin. Chloe rubbed it with the pad of her thumb, cocked her head, and read haltingly, "*Ali di Luna?*"

The instrument had a soft aura in the moonlight.

Its bow was fastened with little ribbon ties onto the lid. They were crumpled, but held. Its wood stain was much darker than the violin under its varnish, and a small, hand-scrawled card was tied to the frog of it. "*Belladonna letale,*" she realized, "this bow wasn't made for this violin."

She lifted the violin out and examined it. But it was... all right. The strings were a little loose, she tightened them gently at the pegs. There was no shoulder rest, but she had an extra at home. Inside her head she was thinking of where her extra fine tuners might be situated.

Chloe meandered the violin and bow out into the secret room.

There Chloe set the thing on her shoulder and had to duck down to the cloth she laid where a chinrest would normally sit. There was no rosin either, but the bow made a soft, off-tune sound in response to her finger's attempts at harmonics. A sound quite like a sleeper, waking up.

Her case still had rosin. And a tuner. Chloe sat down on her heels on the floor in the next room, unaware of an audience as she wiped down this newcomer to the world, *Ali,* and its dark bow. She checked the hair on the bow and the strings and in the half an hour it took for the food to arrive, Chloe nursed warmth and life into the violin she handled and breathed upon.

Finally, she made a little exhalation. It lay out before her on an open coat, its coffin case tucked inside her modern one. And the glowing violin was *ready.*

"*Belladonna letale*. It's Italian for," Graeme settled down on her left to show her his phone results. "*Deadly Nightshade*. How cool is that?"

Chloe lifted the bow, caught up the violin, and set it on the roll of chamois on her shoulder. She took a deep breath and played her first notes. The bow... tingled in her fingers, rock steady. The violin felt warm. And the most soulful, rounded lowing of Sibelius Violin Concerto expanded from the mouths of this instrument with Ds and Gs fair to making the walls bow outward, or so she imagined. It had gorgeous, open sound like no violin Chloe had played before. She fairly held her breath.

It was like... had a quality like... the voice of a singer. Like it might speak.

"Whoa," Molly exhaled.

The room flooded with a delicious mingling of scents—fresh bread, chicken and peppers, and the confidence of paprika—so Chloe had to glance upward. Her mother stood in the doorway with two full white bags with red-scripted *Nosh* in two languages on the side. "But *zeeskeit* you said your violin was *stolen*." Her brows pulled up in the center of her forehead over care-reddened eyelids.

Chloe's voice swelled with gratitude, "No, Mom. This violin isn't mine. We just found it in this room. But it's so beautiful, isn't it?"

"It is. And you'll take it home and play it," said Ms. Chang. "It needs care."

Although she tried not to, Chloe passed the bow to her left hand with the violin, curled the right over her face, and cried with relief.

IT WOULD BE THE SIBELIUS.

She knew it best, found it the most moving, and the swells within that song rang through her home with such grandeur that the police might have been summoned, if the story of what had become of Chloe Barin's 500-dollar instrument *hadn't* been through the *entire neighbourhood* by then. She worked so late that, on Friday, her mother had elected that Chloe sleep in. The pain of such a violation—to have a part of Chloe *stolen*—had been weighty enough that the entire family suffered it.

But Chloe found herself burning to go to practice at the end of the day. Her energy was *high*, even with all the work she'd put in on the new violin the night before. She left at noon, endured Jake riding the bus with her, and hugged him before she climbed out to go into L 'école des Cordes. He held up his phone as she stood, "Any trouble—*any at all*? I'm across the street in the coffee shop. My ringer is on. Got that, beanpole?"

"Thanks, Jake." She left the bus and ambled up the steps toward her school.

Only when she neared the doors did the frantic oboe player who'd helped her tune so many times before, rush to her side. "You need to come with me!"

"What?" She shook herself.

"*Chloe*, the *final auditions* are today. Didn't you see the posting?" The oboe player scanned her stunned, and then embittered, expression and said, "Never mind. The others have been practicing all day in the upstairs. You've gotta go."

"I... I practiced almost all night," she told him and hurried after. "But I can't go to the room I was assigned. Do you think we can borrow one downstairs?"

"Why?" He asked, but the question was routed by the sudden rush of several first violins and a pianist who hurried over to her.

"She's here?" One gasped.

"Thank God!" The pianist clapped her hands to her cheeks.

"*Why* are you so *late*?" The oboe player led the way toward Maestro's office.

"No, I can't sign in." Chloe caught his elbow and it seemed to calm him. "We need to see if I can use the art room to warm up. Or somewhere away from the others. I can explain."

"You don't understand, Chloe. You have to sign in and go upstairs, *now*. The Maestro-"

The door to Maestro Keng's office opened and let him into the hallway, and when he saw her, he heaved a sudden sigh. "I've been looking for you. Your phone number isn't in the records, did you know?"

Chloe gave a sudden bubble of laughter. "We moved above my uncle's restaurant."

Maestro's smile was wide, "Ah. Okay. I thought you might have given up, Ms. Barin, and broken Paganini's heart. Wherever he is. In the firmament." He turned in place, found her name on the list, and marked her down as *Present* himself. Then he passed over the pen so that she could initial under the column for 'Audition / 1ˢᵗ Chair'.

"I had a setback, it's true. It almost stopped me cold, I admit." Chloe released the dangling pen and wiped her hand against her skirt. "But the truth is *I'm ready.*"

"Wonderful. You're here just in time to prove it." He glanced over the startled faces of the other players, more than a touch perplexed by their numbers and expressions. "And what... ever the rest of you are doing down on the ground floor. You can all walk with me to the classroom."

"I'd rather practice in the downstairs-" began Chloe.

"Practice?" Maestro Keng chuckled. "The auditions start in 12 minutes. I would suggest you walk directly there now. You'll have time to tune before you begin. Do you know what piece you're playing? I posted a list on my door yesterday."

Again, she'd had no idea. "Sibelius Violin Concerto?" She noted.

"The last audition I heard with that piece the violinist tired and played triplets in the third section." The Maestro winced. "But... it's an exhausting piece, emotionally and physically. The sound intensity must be right, the double stops, chords, and up-bow staccato must be *authentic*. It is a musical feat, Miss Barin. There is *nowhere* you can fake it in Sibelius, and my expectations are *high*."

Chloe said, "Good."

When they reached the upstairs hall, her fellow players fanned out in front of her. From her vantage at the back of the group, she could see Kendrick and Carnelia joking and laughing in the hall. But Momo stood alone to check her watch, her body restless and shifting.

The tall girl glanced around and only stopped when she caught sight of Chloe. She turned her body in place and made a soft, sad nod in greeting. Kendrick and Carnelia, perfectly confident, went into the orchestra's practice room.

Momo wiped an eyelid as Chloe met her in the hall. "Ken and Carne were talking like you'd bowed out."

"They tried to make me. But they failed." Chloe's head cocked at the other girl. "What happened to you yesterday? With the Headmistress and your parents?"

"I told my dad," Momo peered down at the tips of her black pumps, "if he bullied my way to the first chair... that I would quit school. And he *backed down*." Her almond brown eyes were damp and friendless as she glanced back up at Chloe.

"No. *No.* You won't quit school," Chloe told the other girl. "In fact, stay after, whatever happens. We can practice Paganini No.1 together. I know a place."

She pulled in a breath. Her nude-painted lips pressed down, but Momo nodded. Her voice was clouded with gratitude as she said, "I will."

They walked in together and both Kendrick's and Carnelia's expressions betrayed shock.

When Chloe unzipped one case to take out her violin, Momo sucked a breath. "Oh, you got a new violin. It's beautiful." She bent over the coffin case. "*Ali di Luna.* It's Italian for *Moon Wings.*"

Because *Momo* spoke *Italian.* Chloe grinned as she tested her wooden shoulder, and chin rests. She hefted *Belladonna letale*—the lethal bow— and did some final adjustments in accordance with the oboe *A* she heard spiral above the room.

"Miss Barin? Step up, please," Maestro directed.

Chloe stopped beside the podium where Maestro nodded in greeting. The orchestra awaited their first signal to play, but she would go first.

Chloe readied *Deadly Nightshade* over *Moon Wings,* conscious of the instrument staring down her foes. Chloe paused in the silence, to glance at the pale faces of Carnelia and Kendrick. "Once I'm done here? *I want my violin back.*"

Carnelia's mouth dropped open. Beside her, Kendrick flinched.

When Chloe lowered her deadly bow, the velvet notes made people suck in breaths and stare in wonderment.

The violin murmured promises when Chloe began.

ABOUT THE AUTHORS

TRACY EIRE has been a professional writer for almost a decade writing to a variety of needs, from the magazine Beautiful Bizarre, to collaborations with artists like Jenny Boot. In the mid-2000s, she started her art career and fiction publications. An oil painter with interest in watercolour painting, she was creatively influenced by her childhood home of Newfoundland. The wildness, mysticism, and kindness of this Northern island home just a step out of time, translated into optimism and depictions of light in art. The stamp of those wild climes and pagan survivals became strong impulses in her writing. They can be seen from her rich cast of mystical characters, to the haunting moments we all experience to one side of the flow of normal life, captured in her books. A seasoned writer, she's neurodiverse. Overcoming her disabilities with grit and flexibility creates a highly individual point of view in her work.

Please visit her at tracyeire.site

EMBER FANE has hung a sign above her stories that says, "Read at your own risk." While her humorous side often sparkles, not even she knows what haunted chasm or labyrinthine alley her stories might twist along. Anywhere from the black between the stars through fifty shades of fae, she tells stories of many different hues under the science fiction and fantasy umbrella.

She loves to hear from her readers via emberfane@gmail.com. You can sometimes find her on Twitter @EmberFane

ELIZABETH KNOLLSTON has always been an avid reader of science fiction and fantasy. Now she works on turning her vivid imagination of alien worlds, long lost secrets of the universe, mystical realms and the obligatory dragon into stories of her own. Often blending religious questions and an abiding love for archeology into the driving forces behind her worlds. When not daydreaming about why the local pet store doesn't carry baby dragons, or being a part of a manned mission to Mars, Elizabeth teaches therapeutic riding, spends time with her dog, works in the garden, and loves giving back to the community.

HEIDI MOONE writes things. She says, "I've started to publish some of these things to share them with others. I like writing stories about fantastic places and the magic in the everyday world. I've been reading, and writing, from an early age, and I come from a tradition of oral storytellers, in rural Newfoundland. I love the written word, and it's my favorite medium to communicate my ideas to anyone looking for a new world to explore, and new people to meet along the way."

Please visit her at **heidimoone.com**

KARLI STITES is a tech nerd by day (and also by night). Faced with an overload of creativity that had nowhere to go, she started writing sci-fi and fantasy novels. Karli published the first book in her debut series in 2019, and her young adult romance space opera trilogy, Synchrony Souls, will be completed soon. A lover of all things fantasy and mythological, she recently embarked on a new writing journey, diving into a dragon world full of mystery and magic. The first book in her fantasy dragon shifter series, *Rise of the Drakoni,* will release at the end of 2021.

Find out more about her current books and keep up to date on her upcoming releases at <u>karlistitesauthor.com.</u>

EDITOR N.D. GRAY once dreamed of being an astronaut. Now, she writes characters who reach for the stars, and fills their stories with magic, mayhem, and moonlight.

When she's not writing, she works full time as a caregiver specializing in adults with I/DD, hangs out with the pup pack, and enjoys several creative pursuits, including acrylic painting.

Please visit her at <u>ndgray.com</u>

FOR MORE INFORMATION
PLEASE VISIT US AT
bit.ly/minithology